THE SHARK-Headed BEAR-Thing

LOOK OUT FOR MORE

AMAZING MONSTERS,

TOTAL HEROICS

AND A BIT OF RUNNING AWAY

IN

The Swivel-Eyed
Ogre-Thing

The Moon-Faced
Ghoul-Thing

THE SHARK-Headed BEAR-Thing

BARRY HUTCHISON

illustrated by
CHRIS MOULD

nosy
crow

First published 2015 by Nosy Crow Ltd
The Crow's Nest, 10a Lant Street
London SE1 1QR
www.nosycrow.com

ISBN: 978 0 85763 269 2

Nosy Crow and associated logos are trademarks
and/or registered trademarks of Nosy Crow Ltd

Text © Barry Hutchison, 2015
Cover and inside illustrations © Chris Mould, 2015

The right of Barry Hutchison and Chris Mould to be identified as the author
and illustrator respectively has been asserted.

A CIP catalogue record for this book is available from the British Library.

Printed and bound in the UK by Clays Ltd, St Ives Plc.

Papers used by Nosy Crow are made from wood grown in
sustainable forests.

1 3 5 7 9 8 6 4 2

FOR MUM.
Off on the last
great adventure.

B. H.

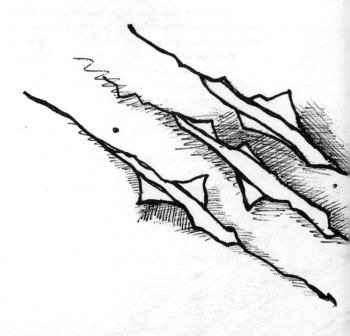

chapter One

Benjamin Blank was having a brilliant dream about kicking a giant up the bum when the world began to tremble. His eyes peeled open and he sat up on his horsehair mattress. The floorboards beneath him were rumbling and shaking.

"Earthquake," he whispered, then he yelled,

1

"Yes!" and punched the air. He'd never been in an earthquake before.

The rumbling stopped as suddenly as it had started, and he realised it probably wasn't an earthquake after all. There was silence for a moment, followed by a loud *boing*. Something shot into his bedroom through the wooden floor, then punched a hole in the thatched roof on its way back out again.

"Sorry!" called a voice from below. "My fault. Breakfast's ready!"

Ben clambered free of his knot of blankets, stretched, then slid down the spiral metal staircase that led into the room below.

A huge contraption filled one half of the circular room. Cogs clanked on the front of it. Steam hissed from little chimneys and water

THE SHARK-Headed BEAR-Thing

bubbled along narrow pipes. Somewhere, hidden in the inner workings, a chicken clucked impatiently. Ben hung back and eyed the machine warily.

"I built it while you were asleep. I call it the Automated Breakfast Producing Device," said Uncle Tavish, who'd never had a knack for catchy names. He stepped out from behind the thing and waved the mechanical arm he'd made for himself after he lost one of his own ones. It was twice as big as his other arm, and the movement almost made him fall over. "Watch this," he said, and he cranked a handle on the machine's side.

The cogs turned, the steam hissed and the chicken *quacked* in a very un-chicken like way. A small brown oval fired out from somewhere

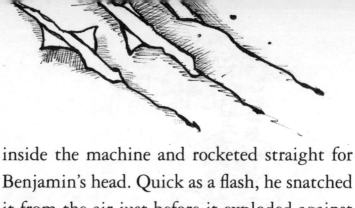

inside the machine and rocketed straight for Benjamin's head. Quick as a flash, he snatched it from the air just before it exploded against his face.

"An egg," Ben said, then he felt his fingers start to burn. He tossed the egg up and began to juggle with it. "Ouch, ouch. Hot, hot!"

"Well of course it's hot. Who'd want to eat cold eggs?" Tavish thought about this. "Unless at a picnic, perhaps. Or pickled eggs, obviously, mustn't forget them." His eyes lit up. "Ooh, an Automated Egg Pickling Device. I must write that down."

"Still hot!" yelped Ben, flicking the egg from one hand to the other.

"Ah yes, sorry," said Tavish. His mechanical arm *whirred* and the metal hand clamped shut around the egg. The shell splintered and a gooey blob of yellow yolk hit the floor with a *plop*. "Whoops," Tavish said. He opened a hatch at his elbow and turned a brass key inside. "Not to worry. Needs a little adjusting, that's all."

Ben pointed up to the hole in the ceiling.

THE SHARK-Headed BEAR-Thing

"Was that an egg, too?"

"Hmm? Oh, no. I thought you might fancy some toast. Haven't quite perfected the pop-up mechanism."

Benjamin stared at the ceiling and up through the hole in the roof beyond. He thought his uncle had perfected the pop-up mechanism a little *too* well.

"Milk?" offered Tavish, pulling down a lever. From inside the machine there came a *moo* of surprise.

"Uh, no," said Ben. "I'm fine."

"Oh. Right. Suit yourself," said Tavish, releasing the handle. Even over the bubbling of the water, Ben heard the cow sigh with relief.

Tavish turned and continued tinkering with

7

the machine. Ben sat at the little wooden table over near the furnace and watched his uncle at work. Tavish was the blacksmith for the village of Lump, but when he wasn't shoeing horses or making swords he was building... things. Some of the things worked. Most of them didn't. Tavish didn't seem to mind either way.

He was small and scrawny for a blacksmith, but his mechanical arm gave him more than enough strength to do the job. It made him so strong, in fact, that the first time he'd tried to shoe a horse while wearing it, he'd accidentally hurled the animal thirty metres into the air. Luckily, he had been able to catch it again. Or most of it, at least.

"I thought I might head out to Kincaid's

THE SHARK-Headed BEAR-Thing

Cave today," Ben said.

"Hmm?"

"Yeah. There's been an ogre spotted."

"Has there? Has there indeed?" mumbled Tavish. He pulled a pipe from the machine and peered into it. A gurgle of dirty water splashed him in the face and he quickly put the pipe back.

"Just a little one," said Ben. "But it's a start."

"Everyone has to start somewhere," nodded Tavish. He slid open a panel in the contraption and a dozen feathers flew out and stuck in his scraggly beard.

"So can I go?" said Ben.

Tavish turned to him and blinked. "Hmm? Go where?"

"To Kincaid's Cave. To fight the ogre."

"Fight an ogre?" gasped Tavish. "At your age? That sounds very dangerous!"

Ben nodded. Of course it was dangerous.

THE SHARK-Headed BEAR-Thing

That was the entire point.

"No, I'm afraid not," said Uncle Tavish. "Too risky. Maybe another time."

A knock at the door interrupted them before Ben could argue. "Not open yet," called Tavish. "Come back later."

The knocking came again, louder this time.

"No, later than that," Tavish shouted. "Come back in an hour."

This time the knocking seemed to shake the whole hut. Benjamin jumped up and pulled the door open. A girl stood there, her clenched fist poised to knock again. She was much shorter than Ben, and was dressed in a green robe with the hood pulled up.

"We're not ope—"

"I'm looking for the warrior," the girl told

11

him. She stood on her tiptoes and tried to peep over Ben's shoulder.

"The warrior?"

"Yes. Is he here?"

Ben straightened his back and puffed out his chest. "*I* am a warrior," he said.

The girl tutted and shoved him aside. "Yes, very funny." She marched past Ben and stopped in the middle of the room. Tavish couldn't work out whether to smile or frown, so he did both at the same time.

"Hello," he said. "Can I help you?"

The girl dropped to one knee and bowed her head. "Mighty warrior, Tavish the blacksmith, I have come seeking your help."

Tavish shuffled nervously. "Uh … mighty warrior? I think you may have me mixed up

with someone else."

"Me, probably," said Ben, but the girl ignored him.

"Are you not Tavish the warrior blacksmith, former soldier in the king's army? Was your arm not lost in service to these lands?"

Tavish scratched his nose. "Yes, I was in the king's army, certainly. I wasn't exactly a *soldier* as such, though. I was in a more … specialised division."

"Catering," said Ben. "He was a chef."

"A *chef?*" the girl spluttered. She pointed at Tavish's mechanical arm. "Well … how did you do that, then?"

Tavish glanced down at the arm, as if only now remembering he had it. "Oh, that. Chopping onions."

The girl stared at him in silence. Tavish gave a shy cough. "They were quite *large* onions."

For a long moment, no one spoke. Then the girl drew herself up to her full height — which wasn't much. "Well, that's just great, isn't it? Three days it took me to get here, and what do I have to show for it? Feet full of blisters and a one-

THE SHARK-Headed BEAR-Thing

handed chef. Brilliant."

Her shoulders slumped. "Well, that's it then," she said. "You were our last hope. There's no one who can stop the monster now."

Benjamin's ears twitched. *Monster. She needed someone to stop a monster.* He ran his fingers through his messy hair, then cleared his throat noisily. When the girl didn't turn around, he tapped her on the shoulder. She finally turned to him and sighed.

"What is it?"

"You're looking for a warrior?" said Ben. He bowed slightly. "You've found one."

The girl snorted. "You?"

"I'm probably the toughest warrior you've ever met."

She looked him up and down. The rough tunic he wore looked a size and a half too big for his skinny body, and his bare legs were covered in grass stains and grazes. "I doubt that," she said.

THE SHARK-HEADED BEAR-Thing

"I'm dead tough. Honest, it's like I'm practically invincible!"

There was a high-pitched whistle from somewhere far above. It quickly grew louder, then the ceiling directly above Ben gave a *crack*. Something flat and burnt-looking punched through the wood, *boinged* off the top of his head, then *clonked* to the floor. They all looked down at it. It was a slice of blackened bread.

"Toast's ready," Ben slurred, then he toppled forwards like a falling tree and landed with a *thud* on his face.

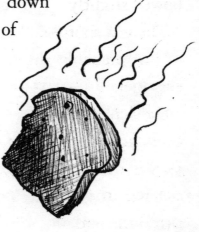

chapter Two

Ben opened his eyes to find Tavish peering down at him. A smile of relief spread across the blacksmith's soot-stained face.

"See," Tavish said, "I told you he wasn't dead."

The girl appeared behind him, stretching up to see over his shoulder. She looked down

THE SHARK-Headed BEAR-Thing

at Ben. "I don't know. He still looks a bit dead to me," she said, then she broke off a piece of toast and crunched it noisily.

Ben got to his feet. He thought he could feel a lump forming on the top of his head, but he resisted the urge to reach up and check. "How long was I knocked out for?" he asked.

"Ten minutes," said the girl. "You were knocked out for ten minutes."

"Oh," said Ben.

"By a slice of bread," the girl continued.

"Right," said Ben.

"I mean … I'd hate to see how you'd fare against a whole loaf. Some warrior you are."

"It caught me off guard, that's all!" Ben protested. "And I'm an amazing warrior."

The girl tried to gnaw off another piece of

19

the blackened toast, but her teeth couldn't get through it. "Sure you are," she said, then she turned and headed for the door. "Thanks for the toast," she called to Tavish.

"Don't mention it," replied Tavish, who was back tinkering with his machine again. "Good luck with your monster situation."

"Thanks," said the girl. She was almost at the door, and Ben could see his dreams of monster-

THE SHARK-Headed BEAR-Thing

hunting slipping away. He put a hand on one of the levers of the breakfast machine.

"Hey wait!" he called, and the girl stopped.

"What now?" she asked, and she turned around just as Ben pulled down on the handle. Cogs turned. The machine rumbled. A chicken went *quack*, and a high speed oval shot from a tube and streaked across the room in the girl's direction.

Before it could reach her, the egg

exploded and a spray of hot yolk and gooey white splattered down on to the floor. The girl looked up to see Ben holding a home-made catapult. He lowered the weapon slowly, then tucked it back into the belt

of his shorts.

The girl glared at him,
then down at the soggy mess on the floor.
Eventually, she said, "What's your name?"

THE SHARK-Headed BEAR-Thing

"Benjamin. My friends call me Ben. You?"

"Paradise. Paradise Little," said the girl.

Ben snorted out a laugh. "Ha! Good one."

"What's so funny?" the girl glowered.

"Oh," said Ben. "You were being serious. I just thought, with you being so … well … *little* and everything…" He saw the angry expression on the girl's face. "It's a great name. Really suits you."

Paradise's eyes narrowed. "Right then, *Benjamin*, if you think you're up to it, you're welcome to try and take on the monster that's been terrorising my village."

"Excellent!"

Tavish's head popped up from behind his machine. "Say what now?"

"She says I can go fight the monster!" Ben

23

said. "How great is that?"

"Not great, not great at all," clucked Tavish. "It's not safe to fight monsters at your age."

"So ... what age *is* it safe to fight monsters at?" Ben asked.

This caught Tavish off guard. The blacksmith floundered. "Well ... I mean ... never. There's no age when it's safe to fight monsters."

"Exactly," Ben said. "So I might as well go now."

"I've recruited loads of other warriors, too," Paradise added. "I've spent weeks rounding up the bravest monster hunters in the land."

"See, so I wouldn't even have to do anything," Ben said. "I could just watch."

Tavish looked unconvinced. "I don't know..."

THE SHARK-Headed BEAR-Thing

"Come on, Uncle Tavish, it's just one little monster," Ben pleaded.

"Big monster," said Paradise.

"It's just one big monster."

"Huge, actually."

"You're really not helping," Ben said.

Tavish ducked down behind his machine. There was a rattling and clanking as he clambered out through a gap at the bottom. His robotic arm *whirred* as he hoisted himself upright. For a long time he just stared at Ben, and there was sadness in his eyes.

"Well, I suppose it had to happen sooner or later," Tavish said quietly. "I can't hold you back forever."

"You mean … I can go?" Ben said.

"You can go and *watch*. That's all."

"Brilliant!" cheered Ben, punching the air for the second time that morning. "Will you make me a sword?"

"No," said Tavish. "I won't."

"But…"

Tavish held up a hand – his real one – for silence. "I won't make you a sword because you already have a sword."

"What, that wooden thing I play with?" Ben asked. He shot a glance at Paradise. "*Used* to play with, I mean. Like *yeeeeears* ago." He laughed a little too loudly. "I don't even know where it is these days."

"Hanging from your belt," Paradise said.

Ben looked down at the wooden weapon dangling from his waist. "Oh yeah," he mumbled, his cheeks turning a shade of pink.

THE SHARK-Headed BEAR-Thing

"Er ... I wonder how that got there."

"No, not that one," said Tavish. "You have another sword. A sword I should have told you about years ago. Come this way," he said, and he made for a small door tucked away at the back of the workshop.

The door was locked. The door was *always* locked. Ben had never seen it open, and although he had tried to get through it many times when he was younger, he'd stopped

thinking about it in recent years.

There was a series of clicks as Tavish turned

a dial on his robotic arm. With a hiss of steam his metal hand folded in on itself like a particularly chunky piece of origami. The fingers flipped and twisted until they formed the shape of a key.

Tavish hesitated, and Ben thought his uncle might be about to change his mind. But then the key slid into the lock, and the door opened with a low, ominous *creak*. Rough stone steps led down into absolute darkness.

"A basement? We've got a basement?" said Ben. "What do you keep down there?"

Tavish turned. His face was grave and serious. "Secrets," he said, then he stepped through the doorway and was swallowed by the dark.

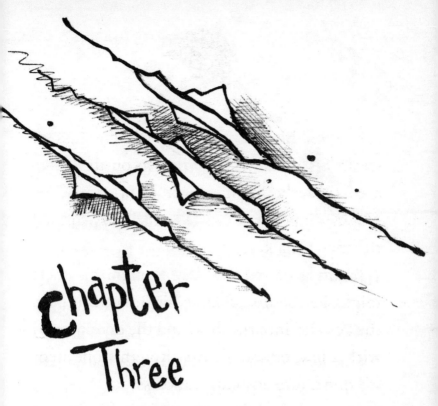

chapter Three

Ben clumped down the steps, shrugging off the darkness. Paradise stuck close behind him, her footsteps soft and silent on the stones. What little light had seeped in through the door had long since faded, and Ben was beginning to wonder just how deep underground they were going.

"Almost there," called Tavish, as if reading his mind. Up ahead, a flame burst into life as the blacksmith lit a torch on the wall.

The flickering torchlight cast an eerie glow across the basement. Actually, "basement" was too generous a description. It was really little more than a deep hole in the ground. Worms wriggled in the dirt walls, and roots tangled across the floor. Bugs skittered away from the glow of the torch, and Ben had to fight to stop himself shuddering. Monsters he could handle, but creepy-crawlies were

THE SHARK-Headed BEAR-Thing

another matter entirely. He fixed his gaze on Tavish and did his best to ignore the scuttling bugs all around him.

"I can't believe this has been down here the whole time," he said.

"I love what you've done with the place," Paradise added, her voice muffled by her hand over her mouth. "The smell is a nice touch."

A flicker of a frown crossed Tavish's face. "Oh, does it smell? Sorry, I can't tell. My nose is made almost entirely out of wood." He tapped one nostril. It made a hollow *thonk* sound. "War wound. Got too close to a pan of Brussels sprouts."

"So," began Ben. "This sword, then..."

"Yes, yes of course," said Tavish. He led them over to the far corner of the basement

where there was a large boulder with a piece of cloth draped over it. A wooden chest stood beside the rock, its hinges pitted with rust.

Tavish took hold of the cloth. Before he lifted it away, he took a deep breath and fixed Ben with a solemn stare. "You know that I found you in the wreckage of a wagon as a baby."

"Yes," Ben said.

"You know I adopted you and raised you as my own."

"Yep."

"You know I said I didn't know what happened to your parents."

Ben nodded.

"That last part wasn't strictly true. Over the years I've been able to … piece some bits together."

THE SHARK-Headed BEAR-Thing

"Whoa, wait," said Ben, eyeing up the cloth. "That's not going to be their heads under there, is it?"

"It had better not be," spluttered Paradise.

"Because if you whip that off and there's a couple of heads looking up at me I'm not going to be happy."

"Of course it's not their heads!" Tavish cried.

"I'll be sick if it is," Paradise warned. "I'll be sick right over your shoes."

"It's nobody's head!"

"Or, like, a leg," Ben continued. "Just a horrible bit of leg all stitched together and rotting and…"

"Information!" Tavish said. "I've been able to piece some bits of *information* together."

"Oh," said Ben. He cleared his throat. "Carry on."

"From what I can gather, something attacked the wagon carrying you and your parents, Benjamin. Something big. Something strong. I believe your parents were … taken. But you were left behind. You, and this."

He lifted the cloth away, revealing the ornately decorated handle of a sword. A carving of a frightening clawed creature adorned the hilt. The sword's blade was embedded deep into the rock itself, with only a few centimetres visible between the handle and the stone.

"I've had the carving analysed," Tavish said. "It appears to be the emblem of the Monster Hunter Guild."

"There's no such guild," said Paradise.

THE SHARK-HEADED BEAR-Thing

Tavish gave a slow nod. "Not now. Not in a long time."

Ben felt like the whole basement was spinning and might come caving in on him at any moment. He couldn't believe what he was hearing.

"They were monster hunters?" he gasped.

"My parents were monster hunters?"

"It appears so," Tavish said. "I don't know how the sword got into the stone, but no one has been able to get it out since." He waved his robotic arm. "Even with this thing, it won't budge. Magic, you see?"

He fished in his pocket and pulled out a small rectangular box. He gave it a shake and pointed one of the box's narrow ends towards the sword handle. After a moment, the end of the box folded open. A little wooden bird popped out on a spring, went, "Bloop," then popped back in again.

Ben blinked. "What was that?"

"I call it the Automated Magic Detecting Device," Tavish said. "A single *bloop* means it has detected magic. Two *bloops* means it has

THE SHARK-Headed BEAR-Thing

detected vast quantities of magic."

"What if it gave three *bloops*?" asked Paradise. "What would that mean?"

Tavish thought for a moment. "That would mean that raw magical energy was about to tear the very fabric of the universe apart," he said. "Or that the batteries needed changing."

Paradise frowned. "What are batteries?"

Tavish waved his hand dismissively. "Oh, just a little something I invented. I doubt they'll catch on."

Ben shook his head. "I don't understand. Why didn't you tell me any of this before?"

"I … I don't really know," Tavish admitted. "The Soothsayer High Council told me a day would come when you would be summoned. When you would be called to your destiny."

His eyes went to Paradise. "By a damsel in distress. I just … I wanted to keep you safe until that day came."

"Who are you calling a damsel in distress?" asked Paradise.

"You've spoken to the Soothsayer High Council?" Ben said. He could hardly believe it. The Soothsayer High Council was a group of wise men and women who could tell the future. They travelled around the country, revealing the destinies of those brave enough to ask. Ben had seen them a few times, but he had never worked up the courage to approach them because they were all a bit on the strange side, and they smelled quite strongly of cabbage.

Ben looked at the handle of the sword poking

up out of the stone. "So this is mine?"

"I think so, yes," said Tavish. "The council believes it can be freed only by the right person at the right time. By you, Benjamin. Now."

A hush fell across the basement as Ben took a step closer to the boulder. He looked back, first at Paradise, then at Tavish. "Here goes," he said.

Taking a deep breath, Ben reached out and wrapped his fingers around the sword's handle. A tingle of magical energy tickled up his arm, making the hairs stand to attention on the back of his neck. Images of battles and stunts and high-speed wagon chases buzzed like lightning through his brain as he heaved on the sword and...

Nothing.

"Well go on, then," said Paradise. "We haven't got all day."

Ben pulled again. "It won't budge."

THE SHARK-HEADED BEAR-Thing

"Try putting your foot on that bit," urged Tavish, pointing to a flat part of the boulder.

Ben did as he was told, then pulled until his face turned a worrying shade of purple.

"I think his head's going to explode," Paradise said.

With a gasp, Ben let go of the sword. Slowly, his face returned to its normal colour. "Maybe it's not my sword," he said.

"Maybe," said Tavish, stroking his chin. "Or maybe it's not your time."

"Can you make me one then?" Ben asked.

"If the sword doesn't think you're ready to wield it, then who am I to argue?" Tavish said.

41

"You can use your wooden one for now. Like you said, you'll only be watching the other warriors, anyway, so you shouldn't be in any danger."

"But—"

"I haven't raised you this long just to have you lop one of *your* arms off like I did," Tavish said. "Anyway, I have something else to show you. The third and final thing I found in the wreckage of that wagon."

The rusted hinges squeaked as he opened the lid of the chest. A metal gauntlet lay nestled within. "Pick it up," Tavish urged.

Ben reached in and took the gauntlet. Its surface shone like polished silver. The glove was big and bulky, but as he slipped his right hand inside, it seemed to shrink to fit him perfectly. He balled his fingers into a fist, and suddenly felt like he could punch through solid rock.

"According to the Automated Magic Detecting Device, that gauntlet's a double blooper," Tavish said, his voice a hushed whisper. "I have no idea what it does, but in all my days I've never come across an item so packed with pure magical power."

"Where's the other one?" asked Paradise. "Gloves usually come in pairs."

Tavish shook his head. "There was only this one," he said, then he stared past the children, as if looking back through the mists of time itself. "My studies of this gauntlet began long, long ago, when you were just—"

"That's a lovely story," interrupted Paradise.

"Really. Fascinating. But there's a great big monster ripping up my village, remember?"

"Oh yes, good point," said Tavish. He turned to the boy and tried his best to smile, but tears formed at the corners of his eyes. "Then it's time, Ben," he said, spoiling the moment a bit by loudly blowing his nose on his sleeve. "It's time to face your destiny."

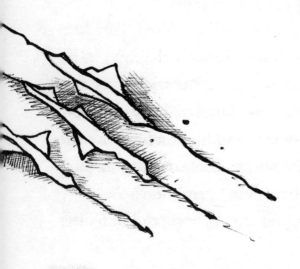

chapter Four

Ben's boots squelched through the mud as he and Paradise hurried along the wide, crowded streets of the village of Lump. The market was already in full swing, and the smell of smoked kippers, fresh bread and barbecued lump-hog swirled in a delicious mist around them.

As they weaved their way through the

throngs of shoppers, voices raised up all around them.

"Morning, Ben!"

"Good to see you, lad!"

"Eat something, boy, you're thin as a rake!"

Ben smiled and waved back at everyone with his metal gauntlet. Then he led Paradise past the final few stalls and out on to the road that ran to the north of the village. The road was long and straight, and stretched out almost as far as the eye could see.

"So what's your village called?" Ben asked, preparing himself for the long hike ahead.

"Loosh," said Paradise.

"What? But that's only twenty minutes away. You said you walked for three days to get to my house!"

THE SHARK-Headed BEAR-Thing

"I did," Paradise admitted. "I got kind of lost."

"You got lost between Loosh and Lump?"

"No, I didn't get lost. I never get lost. I got *kind of* lost."

"For *three days*?"

"Yes!" she said, her face crinkling into an angry scowl. "Do you have a problem with that?"

Ben shook his head. "Nope."

They trudged on in silence for a while. The sun was climbing in the sky, and the trees on either side of the track were alive with the twitter of birds.

"So ... what are you then?" Ben asked.

Paradise frowned. "What do you mean?"

"I mean, are you an elf or something?"

"Why would I be an elf?"

"Just, you know, being so small."

"I'm not *that* small!"

"You're pretty tiny," said Ben.

"I'm nearly average height," Paradise replied.

"For an elf, maybe."

"Elves aren't short, they're tall," Paradise said. "Everyone knows that."

"What? I mean, yeah." Ben forced a laugh. "Of course. Just kidding."

They walked on a bit more.

"So, what, you're just a human being then?"

"Yes!"

"You're an ordinary human being?"

"Yes, of course I am!"

48

THE SHARK-Headed BEAR-Thing

"Not a goblin or a pixie or anything?"

"No!"

Silence fell again. They'd only gone a few more steps when Ben broke it.

"You didn't really recruit loads of other warriors, did you?" he asked. "You were just making that up so Tavish would let me go with you, right?"

Paradise shook her head. "No, I did. I rounded up the roughest and toughest fighters I could find from all over the country."

"Oh," said Ben, his shoulders sagging. "So I will just be watching after all."

"No, you'll definitely get to fight," Paradise assured him.

"Won't the other warriors mind?"

"I shouldn't think so," said Paradise.

"They've all been horribly killed."

Ben's eyes widened. "Really?"

"Of course not," Paradise said, smirking. "I went looking for a great warrior and your house was where I eventually ended up. I asked around whose house it was, and found out about Tavish. I guessed he had to be the warrior I was looking for."

"Him? Nah, don't know where you heard that from," said Ben. "If he cuts his finger he has to go for a lie down. I've fought loads of monsters, though."

"What kinds?"

"Oh, you know," Ben said, after the tiniest of pauses. "Big ones. Bigger ones. Er … other things."

Paradise stopped sharply and sniffed the air.

THE SHARK-HEADED BEAR-Thing

"Do you smell that?" she said.

"Sorry, I think I stepped in something back there," Ben said.

"Not that," Paradise said. "It's sort of a … burning smell, like…" Her eyes went wide. She barged past Ben and broke into a run. "The village!" she yelped. "It's coming from my village!"

They sprinted along the track, clambering over fences and bounding across streams. Paradise was faster, but Ben was better at jumping and climbing, so they were neck and neck as they made the final mad dash to Loosh.

By the time they reached the village, there was almost nothing left. Stone shacks lay in ruins. The burnt wreckage of wooden huts smouldered and smoked. All that remained

was the village well, a trampled vegetable patch, and an elderly donkey in a straw hat.

"*Trolls' teeth*! I've never seen anything like it," Ben said.

"I-I know," Paradise stammered.

"I mean … a donkey," said Ben, "wearing a hat!"

"Not that! My whole village has been destroyed."

Ben's eyes widened, as if he were only now spotting the damage for the first time. "Oh. Right. Yeah, so it has."

Paradise cast her gaze across the wreckage. "They're gone," she said. "Everyone's gone. I'll never see them again."

"Helloooo?" called a voice. Paradise didn't seem to notice.

THE SHARK-HEADED BEAR-Thing

"Mr Thringle from the baker's. Gone," Paradise said. "Bibbly Codd, the goat tamer. Gone."

The voice came again. "Is there someone up there?"

"Old Granny Belcher. Voice like an angel, face like the back of a dog. I won't see the likes of her again," Paradise continued.

"We're down the well!"

"Do you mind?" Paradise snapped. "Some of us are trying to be upset here, and it's not easy with... Wait! The well!"

They dashed to the well and peered into the gloom. A dozen villagers were crammed down there, clinging to the rough stone walls or treading water below. An old woman with a face like the back of a dog let out a cheer when

Paradise's face appeared at the top of the hole.

"Paradise! We're saved," she sang.

"What happened?" Paradise asked. "Was it the monster?"

"It was!" sobbed the woman. "It was horrible."

"It had the head of a shark!" one man cried.

"And the body of a bear!" added another.

"And the tail of a bunny!" said a third. There was a pause. "But a dead scary one."

"What's a shark?" asked Ben.

"*Yaaar*, lad," came a voice from the gloom. "A shark be a big fish."

"That's Captain Swordbeard," explained Paradise quietly. "He used to be a pirate, but now he runs the fishmonger's."

"A big fish doesn't sound too bad," Ben said.

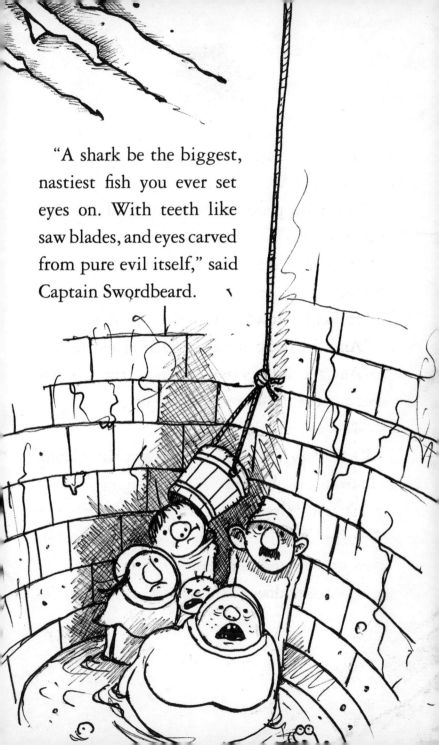

"A shark be the biggest, nastiest fish you ever set eyes on. With teeth like saw blades, and eyes carved from pure evil itself," said Captain Swordbeard.

"Actually, that does sound pretty bad," Ben admitted.

"We'll get you out," Paradise said. Ben turned the wooden handle that lowered the bucket down into the well. When it was close to the bottom there was a loud *THUNK*!

"Ooyah!"

"Sorry," said Ben, and he wound the handle back half a turn. There was a scrabbling and splashing and the rope went tight.

"Ready!"

Ben cranked the handle backwards. After a minute or more of winding in the rope, a man's head rose slowly into view.

The man was short and chubby, with a red face and only a few strands of hair on top. His knuckles were white from gripping the rope, and his whole body trembled as Paradise helped haul him over the edge of the well.

"Mayor!" Paradise cheered. "Are you OK?"

The man did his best to smile. "Oh, don't worry about me, dear," he said. "I'm fine. Just dandy. It takes more than a silly monster to scare the Mayor of Loosh!"

A furious roar split the morning air, and a hulking shape exploded from the woods beside the village.

Squealing in panic, the mayor tried to jump back into the well, but the beast was a frenzied blur of speed. It closed the gap in a flash and slammed into him, all gnashing teeth and slashing claws. The mayor shrieked in terror as the monster scooped him up in one bear-like arm.

Ben drew his wooden sword, but a kick from the mayor's flailing feet caught him on the chin and sent him spinning to the ground, the sword flying out of his grasp.

"I was lying, I *am* scared! I'm proper terrified!" the mayor squealed. "Don't eat me, I'll taste rubbish!"

Ben tried to stand, but his head was fuzzy from the kick and the ground felt like quicksand pulling him down. Through blurred vision he saw Paradise charge at the rampaging monster, her tiny fists raised.

With a desperate kick of his legs Ben knocked her to the ground just as the creature's claws slashed through the air above their heads.

"I chew my own toenails," squealed the mayor. "And I haven't had a bath in months. I'm probably poisonous!"

The beast let out another ear-splitting roar. Ben scanned the ground for his sword.

There! Still groggy, he half crawled, half rolled to the wooden weapon, snatched it up and leaped to his feet.

"Hey ugly, if you want a fight you…"

Ben's voice trailed off. He looked around. Aside from him, Paradise and the donkey wearing the hat, there wasn't another living creature in sight.

The monster — and the mayor — were gone.

chapter Five

"Where is it? Where did they go?" Paradise demanded.

"I don't know," Ben admitted. He cast his gaze across the woods, searching for any sign of the monster. "It was right here."

"You let it get away!" Paradise yelped.

A shaky voice rose up from the well.

"Everything all right up there? We heard shouting."

"And screaming."

"And something about toenails."

Paradise and Ben leaned over the edge of the well again. "It was the monster," Paradise said. "It took the mayor. We're going after him."

Ben looked up. "How?" he said. "We don't know which way they went."

Paradise's eyes met his. "I'll find them."

"Even if you can, that thing looked pretty nasty. It's too dangerous. Maybe—"

THE SHARK-Headed BEAR-Thing

"Now listen to me, *Benjamin*," Paradise said. "I set off three days ago to find someone who could help, and I found you. I don't know why, but I found *you*. You've fought monsters before, you said."

Ben nodded. "Yep," he said, a little too quickly. "I definitely have."

"Then you're the only one who can help me," Paradise continued. "And you wanted to come, remember? So don't you dare go chickening out on me now."

"No, it's just—"

"He's my dad," Paradise said, stopping Ben in his tracks.

Ben stared. "Is he?"

"Well, no," Paradise admitted. "Not really. I mean … sort of. I mean… There's no time to explain. We have to go after him."

Ben nodded slowly, then he pointed down into the well. "What about them? Shouldn't we get them out?"

"Out? No chance! We're staying down here where it's safe."

"OK, well in case you change your mind…" Ben spun the handle that lowered the bucket down into the well.

THUNK!

"Ooyah!"

Ben winced. "Sorry again."

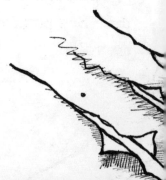

THE SHARK-Headed BEAR-Thing

"Let's go," urged Paradise, and she set off running towards the wall of trees. Ben hurried to keep up with her.

"How do you know the way?" he asked. "They could be anywhere."

"I told you, I can find anything," she replied, not slowing. "There's this sort of compass in my head."

"That must hurt," Ben said.

"Well, obviously it's not a real compass," Paradise sighed. "It's just this ... feeling. I think about what I need to find and it leads me to it. It hasn't let me down yet, and it won't let me down now."

"Although it did take you three days to find me," Ben pointed out. "And I just live down the road."

"I never said it always takes me the most direct route," Paradise replied, not looking back.

They pushed further into the forest, Paradise in front, Ben scrabbling along behind. The trees seemed to close around them, the branches whipping and grabbing at them as they hurried on. The canopy of leaves overhead blocked out the sun, casting the forest floor into deep shadow.

"So the mayor's your dad, then?" Ben called, tripping and stumbling through a tangle of roots.

"Yes," Paradise replied. "No. Sort of. It's a long story. He took me in when I was a baby and looked after me."

"Hey, you're just like me!" said Ben.

THE SHARK-Headed BEAR-Thing

"Ha! You wish."

Paradise ducked a low-hanging branch and clambered over a fallen trunk. The forest rose up around them in all directions, but Paradise raced on.

"Almost there," she said.

The forest seemed to be thinning a little. The trees were no longer packed so tightly, and shafts of sunlight poked through the leaves above.

Paradise began to run faster and Ben had to work hard to close the gap. He was only a few metres behind her when he saw her dash past the final few trees and out of the forest.

"Stop!" she cried, but Ben was running too fast. He exploded from the forest, headed straight for the edge of a deep ravine. His

THE SHARK-Headed BEAR-Thing

boots skidded on the mossy ground. The edge came up quickly. There was no way to stop, he was going to—!

"Saved your life," said Paradise, catching him by the back of his tunic. Ben jolted to a stop with his toes sticking out over the edge. Beneath them was a lot of empty space, followed by a long fall to a river far below. From up there, the river looked like a piece of blue thread tangling its way across a rough stone floor. If Paradise hadn't caught him, it would have taken a good few minutes for him to splatter against the ground.

Slowly, Ben stepped back from the edge. Paradise released her grip.

"What is this?" Ben asked, peering down into the crevasse.

"Deathsplat Canyon. Haven't you been here before?" Paradise asked.

Ben shook his head.

"But it's only a couple of miles from Lump. You said you travelled all over the place fighting monsters."

"I do," said Ben quickly. "It's just I, um, I usually go a different way."

Paradise eyed him suspiciously for a moment, then gave a shrug. "Come on," she said. "The bridge is this way."

It took just a few minutes for them to reach the bridge, although calling it a "bridge" was being quite generous, Ben thought. It was little more than two long ropes strung across the canyon, with planks of wood slung across them. The wood looked damp and

THE SHARK-HEADED BEAR-THING

rotten, and the ropes *creaked* as they rocked back and forth on the breeze.

It seemed like an impossibly long way to the other side of the canyon, where the path led up a hillside and into another forest. The bridge drooped lower in the middle, and Ben was sure he could see spaces where planks had crumbled and fallen away.

"And this is definitely the right way?" he asked.

Paradise nodded. "They're somewhere on the other side," she said. "But I'm not convinced this bridge is safe."

Ben swallowed. "Of course it's safe," he said, doing his best to sound confident. He pointed to a small wooden sign that was set into the ground beside them. It said:

"See, two persons," Ben said. He pointed to himself and Paradise in turn. "One, two. Trust me. It's fine."

THE SHARK-Headed BEAR-Thing

He placed a foot on the first plank. It groaned beneath his weight but held firm. Ben realised he was holding his breath, and let it out in a sigh of relief. "There, see? Nothing to worry about."

They picked their way slowly across the bridge, being careful never to stand on the same plank at the same time. As they got closer to the middle, the wind began to buffet them back and forth. They were almost halfway across when Paradise stopped.

"I think it's going to break."

Ben shook his head. "It won't."

"The wood's rotten," Paradise said. "I heard it creak. It's going to break!"

"It can hold two people, remember?" Ben said. "And you're so small we're probably not

even one-and-a-half. Look."

He bounced up and down on the plank he was standing on. It groaned noisily in complaint and the whole bridge wobbled violently.

"Stop that!" Paradise yelped. "Cut it out, I'm warning you, Ben!"

Ben grinned. "It's fine. Trust me, this wood is *not* going to break."

The wood broke.

One moment Ben was there, the next he wasn't. Paradise gasped and peered over the side of the bridge, expecting to see him tumbling down towards the ground far below.

But she didn't. He was nowhere to be seen.

She crept on to the next plank and looked down through the hole Ben had made. He smiled shakily up at her through the gap. His

THE SHARK-Headed BEAR-Thing

hands were gripping the ropes that held the bridge together, his feet dangling helplessly below him.

"OK, so maybe *that one* was rotten," he admitted. "But the rest of them are fine."

"I'm afraid I would have to disagree with that," said a voice from nearby.

Ben looked along the bridge. There, just a few planks ahead of him, another boy was hanging on just like he was. The boy wore a long red robe with silver moons and stars embroidered on to it. The outfit billowed around him in the stiff breeze.

"Um … hello," said Ben.

"Good morning," said the boy, his voice trembling.

"Who are you?" Ben asked.

"Wesley. Wesley Chant," said the boy. "I'd shake your hand but it's possibly not the best time."

Ben nodded. "Can you climb up?"

"Afraid not," said

THE SHARK-Headed BEAR-Thing

Wesley. "I'm entirely paralysed by fear. I can't even blink," he added, and his voice became a slightly hysterical whisper.

Paradise looked down at the boy through a gap in the planks. "How long have you been hanging there?"

"Let me think," the boy said. He mumbled a few numbers below his breath, then announced: "Since Tuesday."

"What?" said Ben. "But today's Thursday."

"Is it?" asked Wesley. "Already? Doesn't time fly?"

Ben's muscles tightened as he began to haul himself back up on to the bridge. "I'll pull you up. Wait there."

"I shall endeavour to do my best," Wesley replied.

77

"Wait," said Paradise, as Ben clambered back up through the hole. "I've just thought of something."

Ben paused halfway through the gap. "What?"

She pointed to herself.

"One."

She pointed to Ben.

"Two."

She pointed to Wesley.

"Three."

"Oh," said Ben, remembering the sign. "Bum."

And then, with a loud *snap,* the bridge began to fall.

Chapter Six

Paradise screamed. Wesley whimpered. Ben moved.

He hauled himself through the hole, spun, and made a grab for Wesley. The ropes had snapped back near the start of the bridge, meaning the whole thing was swinging down, down, down, like a pendulum, faster and

faster, building up speed with every second that passed.

"Give me your hand!" he bellowed.

"What's the p-point?" Wesley stammered.

Ben's gloved hand caught Wesley by the front of the robe. A tingle crept through the fingers of the gauntlet and up his arm, and he found he could lift the boy without any effort.

"Because," Ben cried, pulling Wesley through the hole, "you don't want to be on that side when we hit the—"

"Wall!" shrieked Paradise.

There was no time for Ben to brace for the impact. As the bridge slammed against the canyon wall his grip slipped and he began to fall. He hit something almost

THE SHARK-HEADED BEAR-Thing

immediately, and it was only when that something started shouting at him that he realised it was Paradise, who had been holding on to one of the ropes.

"Oh, well, thank you *very* much!" she said, as all three of them tumbled down, the wooden boards of the bridge whipping by in a blur of brown.

"Grab my leg!" Ben cried, his voice barely audible over the howling wind and the screaming Wesley.

Paradise twisted and threw out an arm. Her fingers brushed against Ben's boot, but then the wind took her again, flipping her over in a full somersault.

"Grab my leg!" Ben called again.

"I'm trying!"

"Well, stop trying and *grab it*!"

They were almost at the bottom of the dangling bridge. Another few seconds and there'd be no hope of survival.

They had just one chance.

Ben felt Paradise's arms wrap around his leg. Wesley was above him, his billowing robe slowing his descent, but not by much. This was it. It was now or never!

With a roar of determination, Ben grabbed one of the planks

THE SHARK-Headed BEAR-Thing

with both hands. His arms jerked tight. A jolt of pain tore across his shoulders, his grip on the wood slipped, and they were falling once more.

Gritting his teeth, Ben grabbed for another plank. The rotten wood flaked away beneath his fingers. Ben flailed wildly in mid-air, then caught hold of the plank below. It held fast. That just left…

"Wesley!" Ben cried. Holding on to the bridge with his left hand, he swung out with the right. As the gauntlet touched Wesley again the tingle in Ben's fingertips returned. It snaked up his arm and through his aching shoulder, easing the pain. His grip tightened. His muscles tensed. And Wesley's descent came to a sharp, sudden stop.

"Ooh! Ooh! Wedgie! Wedgie!" Wesley grimaced. He flapped about like a badly injured bird for a moment, until his spindly fingers found the edge of the plank Ben was holding on to. He clung to it like a limpet, his face pressed tight against the wood.

Ben stared in wonder at the glove for a moment, then turned his attention back to the situation at hand.

"Paradise, you can let go of my leg now," he said. "Grab on to the bridge."

"What bridge?" Paradise asked. Ben looked down and realised he and Wesley were hanging from the lowest plank. Below them was nothing but a drop to certain death. "Well, don't just dangle there, get climbing," Paradise said.

THE SHARK-Headed BEAR-Thing

Ben turned to Wesley, who had his eyes screwed tightly shut. "Can you climb?"

"Climb?" Wesley gasped. "What ... up?"

"Well, I don't recommend down," Ben said.

Wesley swallowed. "I may just stay here," he said.

"You can't stay here!"

"Why n-not?" Wesley asked. He nodded at the empty space around them. "Lovely view."

"Can we get a move on?" asked Paradise. "Your feet stink."

"Feel free to let go if they're bothering you," Ben replied. "Wesley says he can't climb."

"Leave him, then."

"What?!" Ben spluttered. "We can't do that."

"He's not our problem. We've got to save the mayor."

"We can't just leave him dangling from a bridge!" Ben protested.

"He was dangling from a bridge when we found him. It's not like he's any worse off."

"I d-don't mind, really," Wesley added. "It's really quite nice down here."

Ben shook his head. "I'm not leaving him."

Paradise gave a sigh. "Right. Fine," she said. "Hey, you. New guy. Look at me."

Slowly, as if the slightest movement might make him fall off, Wesley craned his neck so he could look at Paradise. She shot a fierce glare back at him. "Climb," she said, in a voice that was icy cold. "Climb. Right. Now."

"B-but…"

THE SHARK-Headed BEAR-Thing

Paradise's expression darkened. "Don't make me come up there."

Wesley opened his mouth to argue, but something in the girl's eyes made him close it again. Instead he reached a trembling hand up past the missing plank until it found the next one. Then, with great effort, he began to climb.

As Wesley worked his way upwards, Ben looked down at Paradise. "Thanks," he said.

Paradise rolled her eyes. "Whatever," she said. "Now get us up."

Ben grinned. "Yes ma'am," he said, and with Paradise dangling from his legs, he began to clamber after Wesley.

It took them almost twenty minutes to get to the top. Several times Wesley stopped,

but a sharp word from Paradise urged him onwards. By the time they pulled themselves up on to solid ground, all three of them were exhausted.

They lay on their backs, gasping in air, letting the strength return to their aching limbs. They would have rested there a while, but a sudden rustling from the bushes made them sit up straight.

"What was that?" said Paradise.

"No idea," said Ben.

"We're going to die," said Wesley.

The bush rustled again, louder this time. The children jumped to their feet, Ben's hand gripping the hilt of his wooden sword. There was something dark moving in the foliage, pushing its way out of the bushes towards them.

"What is it?" Paradise asked.

"I don't know," Ben replied.

"We're going to *die*," Wesley squeaked.

With a final push, a short, squat creature with wiry black hair all over its body stepped out of the bushes. It was whistling tunelessly to itself, and beneath one arm it carried a rolled up newspaper.

The creature stopped when it saw it wasn't alone. It looked at each of the children in turn, then slowly jabbed a thumb back in the direction of the bush. "I'd … er … I'd give that five minutes," he said. "That last goat I ate did my stomach no favours."

"A troll," said Paradise.

"A troll?" said Ben.

"*Definitely* going to die," sobbed Wesley.

Ben looked the figure up and down. "That's really a troll?"

"Of course it is," Paradise said. She frowned.

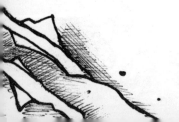

THE SHARK-Headed BEAR-Thing

"You've seen trolls before, haven't you?"

Ben floundered. "Um, yeah. Course I have. All the time."

The troll looked past them, his almond-shaped yellow eyes widening in horror. "Here," he said. "What happened to my bridge?"

"It sort of … snapped," Ben explained.

"Snapped? *Snapped?*"

The troll lurched over to the canyon's edge, his bare feet leaving three-toed prints on the dusty ground. He leaned over and peered down into the crevasse.

"Oh, well that's marvellous that is," he scowled. "That's just marvellous."

The troll took his newspaper out from under his arm, looked around for somewhere to put it, then gave up and tossed it into the canyon.

He rounded on the children, his yellow eyes now little more than narrow slits in his dark face.

"That was my bridge. An' you broke it."

"L-look, we can explain," Wesley stammered. The troll growled at him. Wesley pointed to Ben. "I m-mean … *he* can explain. I don't even know these people!"

The troll fixed Ben with a glare. A wicked grin crept across his face, revealing two rows of rotting teeth. "We're all gonna play a game," he said.

Ben frowned. "What kind of game?"

"Issa good game. Issa *fun* game," the troll said.

"Hopscotch?" asked Wesley hopefully.

The troll flexed his stubby fingers and made

THE SHARK-Headed BEAR-Thing

his knuckles go *crack*. "Nah," he said, and that grin spread further across his face. "Issa little game I made up what I call … Burp or Death!"

The children exchanged a glance. "I think we might skip out on that one," Ben said.

The troll's smile fell away. "You wrecked my bridge," he said. "Either you play Burp or Death, or I gobble you all up right here and now. So," he snarled, his purple tongue flicking hungrily across his teeth, "wossit to be?"

chapter Seven

Ben stepped forward. "I'll play. Leave the others out of it. I broke the bridge."

The troll looked him up and down. "Well, well, ain't you the little hero?" he sneered. The troll wasn't much taller than Ben, but he was wider by far. He loomed over the boy, the foul stench of his breath whistling in and out of

THE SHARK-Headed BEAR-Thing

Ben's nostrils. "All right then, hero. You think you can beat me at Burp or Death? You're on."

"If I win, you'll let us go?"

The troll nodded. "An' if you lose, I gobble you up."

Wesley leaned in. "Just to clarify – by 'gobble *you* up' do you mean just him, or all of us?"

The troll smirked. "All of you."

Wesley's face went pale. "That's a pity." He patted Ben on the shoulder. "Please don't let me die."

"So…" said Ben. "How do we play?"

"The rules of Burp or Death is simple," the troll growled. He gulped down some air, opened his mouth, then let out a short, sharp belch. "Right. Your turn. Is you gonna choose to burp, or is you gonna choose death? An' if

you choose to burp, it has to be louder than mine was."

"So ... what? My choices are to burp or die?"

"That's it," the troll nodded. "Burp or Death?"

Ben glanced back at the others. "Burp," suggested Wesley, as if Ben couldn't have figured that out for himself.

"Yeah, I'll choose to burp," Ben said.

The troll looked a little disappointed. "Oh. Right. Will you?" he said. "You sure?"

"I'm sure."

"Really?" asked the troll. "That your final answer, is it?"

Ben opened his mouth and burped. It was long and loud, and tasted faintly of chicken. "Final answer," he grinned.

THE SHARK-HEADED BEAR-Thing

"Right, can we go now?" Paradise sighed. "His was louder."

"No!" snapped the troll. "That was just the first bit. Now you've got to play my second game."

"What second game?" asked Ben.

"Fart ... or Death!"

"Oh, this is ridiculous," said Paradise. She caught Ben by the sleeve. "Come on, we're going."

"What? But you haven't played Fart or Death yet," the troll protested. "I'll eat you if you don't play."

"What, with those teeth?" Paradise said. "Fat chance. Come on, Ben." She pulled him away from the troll in the direction of the forest.

Wesley hung back, not quite sure what to

do. The troll turned to him. "How about you? Fart or Death? It's fun!"

For a moment, Wesley appeared to consider this. "Well why not?" he said. "I think that would be a smashing way to pass the— LOOK! A BIG THING!" he cried, pointing off to his right. The troll's head whipped round.

"Where?" he asked, but by the time the word had left his lips, Wesley had legged it.

Ben and Paradise were almost at the entrance to the woods by the time Wesley came running past them, puffing and panting, his robe hitched up past his knees.

"Don't go," cried the troll as he lumbered along the path behind them. "One game. I'll go easy on you."

There was a loud *gurgling* sound and the troll

THE SHARK-Headed BEAR-Thing

skidded to a stop. His ape-like hands clutched at his stomach and his eyes went wide. "Oh no," he grimaced. "Not again," and he dived headlong into a nearby bush. A moment later, a sound like damp thunder rumbled out from within the foliage.

"Wow," said Ben. "He'd *definitely* have beaten me at Fart or Death."

Holding their breath, Paradise and Ben pushed on after Wesley. They found him cowering behind a tree trunk. He screamed when Ben tapped him on the shoulder, and it was only by grabbing his robe that they stopped him running away again.

"It's us, Wesley," Ben said.

Wesley straightened up and brushed himself down. "Aha, yes. Of course it is. I knew that." He peered back the way they'd come. "Is it gone?"

Ben nodded. "Yep."

Wesley's nose wrinkled. "What's that smell?"

"Trust me," said Paradise. "You don't want to know."

THE SHARK-Headed BEAR-Thing

Ben shook Wesley's hand. "I'm Benjamin Blank," he said. "She's Paradise Little."

Wesley snorted. "Ha! Good one."

Paradise's eyes narrowed. "What's so funny?"

"Well, I mean, *Little* by name, *little* by nature. Look at you, you can't be any more than … than…" He caught the dark look on Paradise's face, then he coughed quietly. "What a lovely name. Wesley Chant, wizard, at your service."

"You're a wizard?" Ben gasped.

Wesley looked down at his red robes, with all the little moons and stars sewn on to it. "Of course I'm a wizard. Why else would I be dressed like this?"

"For a bet?" Ben guessed.

"No! I'm a wizard. I've got a hat and everything." Wesley reached up and touched

101

his head. "Where's my hat gone?"

"You didn't have it when we met you," Ben told him.

Wesley's shoulders slumped. "Wonderful," he mumbled. "I can't even keep my hat on."

"Maybe you can help us. We're tracking a monster," Ben told him.

Wesley stared at them both in turn, then he waved. "Well, lovely to have met you," he said, turning on his heels. "I'll just be off."

"Oh. Right. Bye then," said Ben, unable to hide his disappointment. "If you do run into the monster, just shout."

Wesley froze.

"We probably won't be close enough to reach him in time," Paradise pointed out to Ben. "Before he gets eaten."

THE SHARK-HEADED BEAR-Thing

"You never know," Ben said with a shrug. "We might manage to get to him before he's torn to bits. If we're lucky."

"Torn to b-bits?" Wesley's eyes scanned the forest ahead of him. Anything could be lurking out there in those shadowy nooks and crannies. He swallowed nervously.

"Change of plan," he chirped, turning back and clapping his hands together. "Tell me about this monster."

"It's been lurking outside my village for weeks," Paradise explained. "Sheep have been snatched. Whole cows have been eaten alive."

Wesley gulped. "Eaten … alive?"

"People were getting scared."

"The cowards," Wesley squeaked.

"Today it attacked. It destroyed the village

103

and took the mayor."

"What does it look like?" asked the wizard.

"It's a real mess," Ben said. "All the buildings are wrecked, the people are hiding down a well, and someone put a hat on a donkey."

"He means the monster, not the village," Paradise sighed. "It has the head of a shark and the body of a bear."

"And the tail of a bunny," Ben added helpfully.

Wesley tapped his finger against his chin. "Head of a shark," he muttered. "Body of a bear."

The cuffs of his sleeves were wide and hung down from his wrists. He reached his right hand inside his left sleeve and rummaged around. After a moment, he pulled out a huge

battered-looking hardback book
and — with great effort — held it
up for the others to see.

"Here we are," he announced. *"Who's Who, What's What, and Why They Do Such Horrible Things to One Another* by Lunt Bingwood."

Paradise shrugged. "So?"

"So Lunt Bingwood was one of the greatest adventurers in history. He travelled the world, battling monsters and writing about them."

Ben's eyes widened. He had never heard of Lunt Bingwood until that moment, but already he was Ben's new number one hero.

"This book details every species of monster he ever encountered – and not just the run-of-the-mill stuff like ogres and goblins and what have you – the more unusual types, too. It tells you everything about them," Wesley explained. He set the book down on a tree stump and began flipping through the pages.

THE SHARK-Headed BEAR-Thing

"Let me see, head of shark… Body of bear…"

He stopped at a page somewhere near the middle and let out a cry of triumph. "Aha! Here we are – head of a shark, body of a bear."

Wesley turned the book so the others could see it. There was a black and white illustration of the monster showing it chewing through a slab of solid rock.

"So what is it?" Paradise asked.

"According to Lunt Bingwood," Wesley said, reading the entry next to the picture, "it's a Shark-Headed Bear-Thing."

Paradise tutted. "And that's the best he could come up with, is it?"

"Yes, names weren't really his strong point," Wesley admitted. He flipped through a few pages at random. "He's got the Owl-Headed

107

THE SHARK-Headed BEAR-Thing

Horse-Thing. The Mouse-Headed Sheep-Thing. The Dog-Headed Dog-Thing." He peered at the illustration more closely. "Although, I'm fairly sure that's just a dog."

"What does it say about our monster?" Ben asked. "Does it tell you anything?"

Wesley flipped back to the correct page. "Aha, yes, here we are. *Shark-Headed Bear-Thing*," he read. "*Avoid*."

Ben frowned. "Is that it?"

"Yes, that's all the advice it has to offer," Wesley nodded. "*Avoid*."

"Not an option," Paradise said. "It has the mayor. We have to get him back."

"But the book," Wesley protested. "Lunt Bingwood knows his stuff. *Avoid*, he says."

"The mayor's her sort-of-dad," Ben explained.

"And that's why we have to catch that monster," Paradise added.

"But that's the exact *opposite* of avoiding," said Wesley. "This is Lunt Bingwood we're talking about. *Lunt Bingwood!*"

"I don't *care*," Paradise told him. She pointed into the darkening woods. "Now I'm going after the Shark-Headed Bear-Thing before it eats the mayor. Are you two coming, or are you too chicken?"

Ben raised his hand. "Coming."

Wesley raised his hand. "Chicken." He glanced sideways at Ben, then let out a sigh. "Fine," he said. "I'll come. But be warned – if I get eaten alive, I'll be holding you two personally responsible."

chapter Eight

Paradise led them through the woods, weaving and zig-zagging all over the place. Once or twice she stopped, looked around, then set off in a completely different direction. Ben had begun to suspect she might be lost.

"I thought you said you could find anything," he said.

"I can."

"Then why haven't you found it?"

Paradise turned on him sharply. "Because sometimes it isn't easy. Sometimes the signal goes all wonky, like when it was supposed to be guiding me to a great warrior and it took me to you instead."

"Hey, I *am* a great warrior," Ben protested.

"Oh sure," said Paradise. "The way the mayor's feet knocked you over like that – really tough."

"It caught me by surprise, that's all!"

"What, like the toast did?"

"I saved your life," Ben reminded her. "It would've splattered you if I hadn't stopped you running at it!"

"I would've been fine!"

THE SHARK-Headed BEAR-Thing

"You would've been lunch!"

"Well, at least I didn't almost run right off a cliff," she said, then she about-turned and carried on walking. It was all Ben and Wesley could do to keep up with her as she weaved her way through the woods.

As they walked, Ben studied his gauntlet. When he'd stopped Wesley falling earlier he'd felt it tingle with power, almost as if it were somehow alive. Now it felt cold and still against his skin. He picked up a rock and tried crushing it, to see if the glove would make him strong like it had back at the bridge. The rock remained intact, though. Whatever magic the glove might possess, it wasn't doing anything now.

They trudged on some more through the

tangled undergrowth, and parts of the forest soon began to look very familiar.

"I've seen that tree before," announced Wesley, as if reading Ben's thoughts. They were striding through a small clearing, where the trees weren't so tightly packed together.

"No you haven't," Paradise insisted.

"I have," Wesley said. "Look, I carved my name on it when Ben stopped for a wee earlier."

They looked at the tree. There, just below head height, was Wesley's name.

"Someone else could have done that," Paradise said.

"Why would someone else carve 'Wesley Chant' into a tree?" Wesley frowned.

"Oh … loads of reasons," Paradise said.

Wesley looked at her. "Such as…?"

With a loud sigh, Paradise sank down on to the forest floor. "Fine," she said, her voice suddenly small. "We're lost. There, I said it. Happy now?"

"Ha, I knew it!" Wesley laughed, before Ben nudged him in the ribs.

They looked down at Paradise, but she turned away from them.

"Are you OK?" asked Ben.

"I'm fine," she sniffed.

"Are you crying?"

"Of course I'm not crying," she said, so sharply that both Ben and Wesley jumped back in fright. "I've got something in my eye, that's all."

"Perhaps I can help us find our way," Wesley said. He rummaged around inside a sleeve

THE SHARK-Headed BEAR-Thing

until he found what he was looking for. The fading daylight glinted off a pair of circular glass lenses. "These belonged to my grandfather," he explained, holding up what looked like two short telescopes attached together side by side. They were made of battered leather with two large lenses at one end, and two smaller ones at the other. "They're called Peepsees."

"What do they do?" Ben asked.

"Watch."

Wesley pressed the smaller end of the Peepsees against his eyes, then turned two small brass cogs that were attached to the leather on either side. With a soft creaking, the end that housed the wider lenses began to rise. Each turn of the cogs raised them higher

and higher, closer to the canopy of leaves above them.

Ben and Paradise watched in wonder as the Peepsees pushed through the treetops and vanished out of sight. Wesley stopped turning the dials, and instead began slowly turning himself on the spot. Ben could imagine the Peepsee lenses up there above the forest, their gaze sweeping the area in every direction.

"See anything?" asked Ben.

"No, not really," Wesley said. He continued to turn, then he stopped suddenly. "Wait!" he whispered. "I do. There's ... something."

"The Shark-Headed Bear-Thing?" asked Ben.

"The mayor?" asked Paradise.

THE SHARK-Headed BEAR-Thing

Wesley shook his head. "N-no. It's... something else. Something big. *Really* big. With eight huge hairy legs and ... *argh*! Its eyes. So many eyes! It's..."

Ben tensed. "Yes?"

"It's..."

"What?" hissed Paradise.

"It's... *It's*..." Wesley blinked rapidly then pressed his eyes back to the lenses. "Oh, wait. It's gone. Thank goodness."

He pushed in both cogs and the Peepsees' lenses quickly retracted down from the treetops. As the device clicked back together, Wesley saw that there, perched on one of the lenses, was a creature with eight hairy legs

and more eyes than he could count.

"Oh, I see. It was a *spider*," he realised, before remembering that he was absolutely terrified of spiders. With a shriek, he hurled the Peepsees off into the trees. There was a thud and a crash and a musical tinkling of glass.

"Well," said Ben, as the last of the tinkling died away. "That's the end of the Peepsees."

Wesley blushed. "I should probably try to find them," he said, taking a step in the direction they'd flown. "They were my grandfather's, after all."

"Yeah. It's going to be getting dark soon," Ben said.

Wesley froze. "Actually, I think I'll just leave

THE SHARK-Headed BEAR-Thing

them. My granddad wouldn't have minded,"
he said. He gulped and took a backward step
towards Ben. "And I feel I should probably
warn you – I'm not a big fan of the dark."

"You're a wizard," Ben said. "What have you
got to be scared of? Aren't you supposed to be
all-powerful and everything?"

Wesley puffed out his narrow chest. "Oh
yes. Yes, very powerful," he said, then the air
left him in one big breath and he seemed to
deflate. "Actually, no," he admitted. "Not
really. I'm just a trainee. *Was* a trainee, I mean.
Level one. I got kicked out."

"How come?" asked Ben.

"You're only supposed to remain a level-one
trainee for the first few weeks."

"How long has it taken you?" asked Paradise.

"Six years," replied Wesley, forcing a smile, "eight months, two weeks, five days. Give or take an hour or so."

"Trolls' teeth," whistled Ben.

"Professor Daniels said I was the the most un-magical living creature he'd ever met. He said he's seen sandwiches with more magical ability than me." Wesley looked down at his feet. "So I probably won't be much help to you, I'm afraid. Sorry."

THE SHARK-Headed BEAR-Thing

"You told us what the monster's called," Ben reminded him. "That was a help."

Wesley shrugged, then slumped down with his back against a tree.

Ben looked up. The glimpses of sky visible through the trees were turning purple. Soon the night would draw in, bringing the darkness with it.

"We should camp here," Ben said.

Paradise and Wesley both raised their heads. "Camp?" squeaked Wesley. "What, outside?"

"We can't, we have to save the mayor," Paradise said. "If I can just concentrate, I can find him. I know I can."

"We'll look again in the morning," Ben said. "I know you're worried about him, but anything could happen in the dark. We could

fall in a hole, get attacked by wolves, trip over an ogre…"

"Right, yes, thank you!" Wesley said. "We get the idea."

Paradise wriggled uncomfortably. She hated to admit it, but what Ben said made sense. Still, she didn't like the idea of abandoning the search.

"He found me when I was about a year old," she said, her voice barely more than a hushed whisper. "I was wandering in the woods, lost and alone. And he found me. I couldn't tell him where I came from, or how I came to be in the forest. All I could tell him was my name. Paradise."

"So what happened then?" asked Wesley.

"He took me back to Loosh," Paradise said.

THE SHARK-Headed BEAR-Thing

"He looked after me and brought me up. He gave me a home, food, clothes… So yeah, he might not be my dad, but he's the closest I've got to one."

"Like Tavish," said Ben.

Paradise nodded. "That's why we can't sit around here, why we have to find him. And I don't understand why we haven't. It should be easy! I can find anything."

"Yeah, I still don't really understand that," said Ben. "How do you find things?"

"When you're at home," Paradise said. "How do you know where your bathroom is?"

"Because I've been there before."

"Yes, but you don't retrace your steps every time, do you? Once you know where it is, you know where it is. You can find it again. Well,

I can do that, but with places I've never been to before. With things I've never seen."

"Really, though?" asked Ben. "I mean … couldn't it just be luck when you find things?" He looked across to Wesley. "Have you ever heard of a magical finding ability?"

Wesley shook his head.

"Yes, *really* and no, it isn't luck," Paradise snapped. She crossed her arms, signalling the conversation was over.

They all sat in silence for a while, listening to the sound of night creeping over the forest. The birds had fallen silent, replaced by the chirping of crickets. From somewhere nearby there came a loud hoot, which made Wesley let out a little yelp of fright.

"It's just an owl," Ben said. "Don't worry."

"I'm well aware it's just an owl," Wesley whispered. "Just an owl with its hooked claws and razor-sharp beak and big, staring eyes!

They can turn their heads right around, you know? *Right the way around.*"

"Relax, it's probably nowhere near us," Ben said.

Paradise jabbed a thumb back over her shoulder. "Twenty-two metres that way," she said, without looking. "Fourth branch from the bottom."

Ben stood up. Keeping low, he tip-toed off into the darkness. Several seconds passed before he returned. "She's right," he said, sounding impressed.

"Told you it wasn't luck."

"Then why can't you find the mayor?" Ben asked.

Paradise's head snapped up. "How should I know? I tried."

THE SHARK-Headed BEAR-Thing

Ben held up his hands. "I know, I know, I wasn't saying anything. It's just ... there must be a reason why you can't."

Wesley sat forwards suddenly. "Paradise, why did you stop here?"

"Ben was having a wee," she replied.

"No, no. He only stopped because you did." He pointed to the tree with his name in it. "And I only carved that because I was sure we'd passed that very same tree several times before and I wanted to keep track. So why did you keep leading us here?"

"I thought I felt something. Like we were close, but then we weren't."

"And yet you brought us back to this exact spot again and again," Wesley said.

Paradise and Ben looked at one another.

"So?" they both asked. "There's nothing here."

Wesley rummaged up his sleeve until he found the same leather-bound book he'd produced earlier. He flipped hurriedly through the pages until he found the picture of the Shark-Headed Bear-Thing. "Look what it's doing," he said.

The others leaned in close, struggling to see the picture clearly in the gloom. "Biting a rock," Ben said.

"Exactly!" chirped Wesley. "And look at the background. What does that look like?"

Ben and Paradise went back to peering at the book.

"A tunnel?" Paradise guessed.

"Precisely! And where might one find a tunnel?"

THE SHARK-Headed BEAR-Thing

Ben leaped to his feet. He stared down at the grass, his whole body suddenly twitching with excitement. "Underground!" he said, then he threw himself into the air as high as he could, and brought both feet down with a slam.

There was a groan from all around the clearing, followed by a sound like a giant bubble going *pop*. In a cloud of dust and soil and rotten bark, the entire clearing collapsed beneath them and they tumbled down into a wide hole in the ground.

When the dust settled and the noise faded, all was still. Then, from out of the darkness, Paradise's voice rose up.

"Will you *please* stop jumping up and down on stuff!"

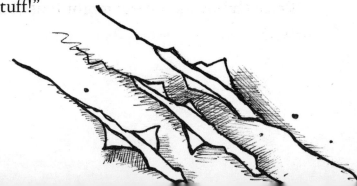

chapter Nine

They had crashed down into a narrow cave. At least, it had probably been narrow to begin with, but now that a large part of the ceiling and walls had fallen in, it was quite a bit wider.

Ben heaved himself out from beneath a pile of dirt, just as Paradise untangled herself from a knot of roots and vines. They looked around

THE SHARK-Headed BEAR-Thing

for Wesley, and eventually spotted a pair of feet poking up from a mound of muck.

Taking a leg each, they pulled until he popped free. Wesley spat out a mouthful of soil and wiped his filthy face on his sleeve. "I was going to suggest we tried to find an entrance," he spluttered.

Ben pointed up to the hole in the ceiling. "Found one," he said proudly.

"Ssh!" hissed Paradise. "Listen."

They listened.

The cave stretched out to their left and right, like a passageway through the Earth. From along the tunnel on their left, Ben could hear the low growling of something monstrous.

"I can't hear a thing," Wesley announced. His voice bounced along the passageway in

both directions.

Paradise gestured for him to be quiet.

"You've got mud in your ears," Ben said, pointing to the side of Wesley's head.

Digging a pinkie finger into each ear, Wesley scooped out some compacted dirt. The sound of the growling reached him immediately. He listened for a moment, nodded once, then tried to pack his ears with soil again.

"Let's go," Ben said, drawing his sword and creeping along the passageway.

"What, *towards* the terrifying monster noise?" Wesley whimpered. "Are you mad?"

"If the monster's this way, that's where we'll find the mayor," Ben replied.

"If he hasn't been eaten already!" Wesley said. Paradise shot him one of her glares.

The SHARK-Headed BEAR-Thing

"Which he *definitely* won't have been," Wesley added quickly.

As they made their way along the tunnel, a reddish glow began to flicker and dance across the stone walls. They tiptoed on, the growling sounds growing louder around them.

At last, they found themselves at the entrance to a much wider cave. A blast of heat hit Ben in the face, pushing him back into the passageway. Steeling himself, he peeped his head out again. A river of slow-moving lava oozed through the cave, winding along a deep trench in the rocky floor.

Ben managed a quick glance around the cavern before the heat forced him to draw back again. "No one there," he said.

Paradise touched her fingers to her forehead.

135

"There's another tunnel on the other side of the lava," she said. "The monster's down there somewhere."

"And the mayor?" Ben asked.

"I'm … I'm not sure. I'm not picking him up."

"Uh, guys," said Wesley.

"There's a bridge," Ben said, glancing out into the cave again.

"Not another one," Paradise groaned.

"This one's made of stone," Ben assured her. "It'll be fine."

"You said that last time," she reminded him.

"Guys?" squeaked Wesley. "I think... I think we should hurry."

Ben turned. "No, we can't hurry, we might slip and..."

That was when Ben noticed the shape moving along the corridor in their direction. It was a big scary-looking shape, but despite its size it was moving really quite quickly indeed. Twin rows of sharp teeth glinted in the glow of the lava.

The roar of the Shark-Headed Bear-Thing shook the walls of the tunnel, threatening to bring more of the roof down on their heads.

Back at Paradise's village Ben had only

THE SHARK-HEADED BEAR-Thing

caught a quick glimpse of the creature. Here, in the narrow passageway with it racing towards them, it looked bigger and scarier than anything he had ever set eyes on. He held his wooden sword out in front of him, trying his best to keep it from wobbling.

"What are we going to do?" asked Paradise, stepping behind him.

"Die horribly," Wesley whimpered.

"Ben?" Paradise said. The floor was vibrating with the thunder of the approaching Bear-Thing, each footstep *booming* along the corridor.

Ben stared. He'd always dreamed of fighting monsters one day, but this one was so big, and so terrifying and...

"Ben!" Paradise said, thumping him on the arm.

He jolted, as if woken from a dream. The monster was fifteen metres away now, and getting closer with each bound.

"Come on, you fight monsters all the time. What do we do?" Paradise demanded.

Twelve metres. Flecks of drool trailed from the thing's gaping jaws.

Ben shook his head. "I don't," he said, his voice coming out as a hoarse whisper. "I've never fought anything before. I made all that up."

Nine metres. Ben saw himself reflected in the creature's dark, dead eyes.

"Ha! I knew it," Paradise cried. "All that stuff about being a great monster hunter, I knew it wasn't true!"

"You s-say that like it's a good thing,"

THE SHARK-Headed BEAR-Thing

Wesley said. "What do we do?"

Six metres. The thing's muscular body tensed, preparing to make one final fatal leap.

"Run!" Ben yelped, shoving Paradise and Wesley out of the passageway and into the wider cave. The heat hit them like a wave of fire, scorching their throats and stinging their eyes. They staggered blindly towards the bridge just as a snarling ball of rage exploded from within the passageway, its fluffy bunny tail twitching with fury.

The Shark-Headed Bear-Thing skidded on the smooth stone. For one short but happy moment Ben thought it was going to plunge into the fiery lake, but then it found its balance and turned, teeth snapping, towards them. There was no way they could all outrun it, no

chance they could all escape.

The picture in the book had made

THE SHARK-Headed BEAR-Thing

the Bear-Thing seem terrifying. Out in the real world it was much worse. Its dense muscles rippled beneath its thick fur. Its curved claws scraped like knife blades against the rocky floor and dark saliva dribbled down its teeth.

But it was the size of it that was the most terrifying thing of all. Even hunched over on all fours as it was now, it was almost three times as tall as Ben. The leathery skin of its shark-head rustled softly as it turned its dark eyes Ben's way.

"I... I can't fight this thing," Ben said.

"Listen to me," said Paradise sharply. "It doesn't matter that you've never fought monsters before. What matters is that you can fight one *now*. And you can. I know you can."

"How?"

"Because I went looking for a brave warrior who could stop this thing and I found *you*," she said. "And I *always* find what I'm looking for, Ben. Always. If you couldn't stop it, I wouldn't have found you. You can do this. You're the only one who can."

Ben stared at her as her words sunk in. The Shark-Headed Bear-Thing advanced, its huge paws padding across the floor.

"Go," Ben said, turning to it. "I'll hold it back."

"What do you intend to do? Let it eat you?"

Wesley squeaked. "That'll barely buy us two minutes!"

"Just go. Find the mayor. I can stop it," Ben said, hoping only he could hear the tremble in his voice.

"You can do this," Paradise reminded him. She slapped him on the arm. "Don't you dare die."

She and Wesley hurried in the direction of the other passageway, and Ben locked eyes with the monster. "You want to eat us? I'm warning you, you'll have to get through *this*," he said, and he held up his sword.

Or, to be more accurate, he held up just the handle of his sword. The rest of it had caught fire and turned to ash when he wasn't looking. Ben stared at the smouldering remains of the

wooden weapon, then back at the Bear-Thing.

With his sword gone, Ben was defenceless. Unless…

The gauntlet! He balled his fingers together, forming a metal fist. He brought it up sharply, hoping the glove's magic would do its stuff.

With a *clank* the gauntlet rattled harmlessly against the Bear-Thing's jaw, and a spasm of pain shot through Ben's fingers and all the way up to his elbow.

"All right," Ben said, pinning his aching hand beneath his armpit. "How about we call it a draw?"

And with that, the monster lunged.

chapter Ten

Ben ducked and rolled. He heard the *whistle* of the Bear-Thing's claws slicing through the air above him, then the *sizzle* of his skin as his bare arm brushed against the searing floor.

"Ooh, ooh, hot, hot," he yelped, then he hurled himself sideways as a huge paw cracked the rock where he had been standing.

THE SHARK-Headed BEAR-Thing

Ben looked up and saw a flash of a cold, dark eye. He stumbled backwards as the monster's jaws snapped shut with a *clack* that echoed around the cave.

"Can't we talk about this?" Ben asked. The monster made another dive for him. It brought both arms up above its head then slammed them down. Ben barely managed to scramble out of the way before the paws crunched against the stone. "I'll take that as a 'no'," he yelped, then he ducked again as the monster's claws slashed at him.

The heat in the cavern made the air shimmer. Ben could feel sweat trickling down his bare legs and into his boots. He squelched as he turned and ran, trying to put as much distance between himself and the monster as possible.

He spun, pulling out his catapult and taking aim with a chunk of volcanic rock. He let fly with the stone. There was a *twang* and a *swish* and a soft *thup* as it bounced harmlessly off the Bear-Thing's shark-head.

Dropping the catapult, Ben turned and ran again. The ground beneath him shook, and he knew the thing was on the move, chasing him, catching up.

He dodged left. A shadow passed over him and the Bear-Thing snarled as it rolled and thudded against the jagged cavern wall.

"And stay down!" Ben warned. The monster flipped itself back up on to its feet. "Or don't. It's up to you," said Ben, and then he was off and running again.

There was no way he could fight this thing

THE SHARK-HEADED BEAR-Thing

without ending up as a lumpy paste on the floor. He had one chance, though. One chance to escape. One chance to survive.

Ben turned towards the river of lava, lowered his head, and charged. At once he felt the sting of the heat on his face. He pushed on. The air around him seemed to bubble and boil. The hazy black smoke swirled up his nostrils and reached down into his lungs.

Paradise's voice echoed around the cavern, screaming at him from every direction at once. "Behind you!"

Ben hurled himself sideways, throwing up his hands to shield himself from the searing heat just as the Shark-Headed Bear-Thing sailed past overhead. Rolling to his feet, Ben watched as the monster tumbled down. Its

brutish limbs flapped frantically as it tried, for the first time in its life, to fly.

And then failed spectacularly.

SPLOONK!

The Bear-Thing performed an almighty belly-flop into the lava, spraying droplets of burning orange in all directions. It let out a final angry *hiss*, then it half-sank, half-melted into the mass of molten rock and was gone.

Ben stared at the spot where the monster had vanished, half-expecting it to come leaping back out.

THE SHARK-Headed BEAR-Thing

It never did. Wiping the worst of the soot from his face, Ben allowed himself a shaky smile.

"I did it," he mumbled. "I fought a monster."

"Told you, now hurry up!" Paradise's voice rang out again. Blinking in the heat haze, Ben scanned the other side of the cave until he spotted Paradise and Wesley in the mouth of another tunnel. "This way," Paradise said. "The mayor's somewhere along here."

Ben tried to speak, but it came out as a series of hoarse coughs.

The sooner he got out of the heat, the better. With a last glance at the Bear-Thing's final resting place, Ben scampered across the bridge and followed the others into the cool dark tunnel.

"That was really quite impressive," Wesley told him. "Really quite heroic!"

"Yes, the way you dropped your sword and ran for your life like that. Amazing," Paradise said.

"I didn't *drop* my sword," Ben told her. "It caught fire."

"And *then* you dropped it and ran for your life," Paradise said, but there was a smile tugging at the corners of her mouth. "You did good. Now let's move on."

"I did do good, didn't I?" he said. "I actually

THE SHARK-Headed BEAR-Thing

fought a proper monster!"

"Yes, but don't keep going on about it," Paradise said. "We still need to rescue the mayor."

Ben cupped his hands around his mouth and shouted into the darkness ahead of them, "Maaaaaayor! Yoo-hoo! Can you hear me?"

"What are you doing?" hissed Wesley. "Something might hear us."

"That's the whole idea," Ben said. He puffed out his chest. "You don't have to worry about the monster any more. I took care of it. Did you see me?"

"We don't need to shout," Paradise said. "I can find him. Follow me."

They moved on. Ten paces later, they stopped again.

"It's quite dark, isn't it?" Ben said.

"Can't see a thing," Paradise admitted.

"We're going to die!" Wesley whimpered. "Oh no, wait, hang on," he added, then there was the sound of him rustling around inside his gaping sleeves.

A moment later a blinding light lit up the passageway, forcing Ben and Paradise to cover their eyes. "Sorry everyone, sorry," Wesley said. "Here, let me just adjust…"

The brightness dimmed. Ben and Paradise blinked away the spots behind their eyes, then turned to Wesley. He was holding a small glass jar by a length of string that was tied to the top of it. The glass was a smoky shade of black, but whatever was inside the jar was powerful enough to still be lighting up thirty

THE SHARK-HeadEd BEAR-Thing

metres of tunnel in both directions.

"It's a sun," Wesley explained.

Paradise frowned. "The sun?"

"No, not *the* sun," replied Wesley. "*A* sun. Just a small one. I won it last year in a contest with a level-three trainee."

Ben looked impressed. "A magic contest?"

"Tiddlywinks," Wesley said.

"Oh."

"I'm really rather good."

Paradise rolled her eyes and set off along the passageway again.

"So you just walk around with a sun up your sleeve?" Ben asked.

"Among other things," Wesley said. "It's amazing what you'll find up a wizard's sleeve. There's stuff even I've never seen before. I had

a whole family of badgers living up there for six months. Didn't know a thing about it. Nice glove, by the way."

Ben held up the hand with the gauntlet. "What, this? Thanks. It was my dad's. Or my mum's. Not really sure which. It's magic."

"Really?"

"Yeah. Not sure what it does, but back at the bridge, when I caught you, I think it made me stronger for a few seconds.

THE SHARK-Headed BEAR-Thing

I've been fiddling about with it since then, but it hasn't done anything else."

A flicker of recognition darted across Wesley's face. "It looks familiar," he said. "Here, could you hold this?"

Wesley passed the jar to Ben. "Don't drop it," he advised.

"Why not? What would happen?"

"No idea," Wesley said. "But I'd rather not find out."

He thrust a hand back inside a sleeve again, then pulled out a book. This book was smaller than the other one, but with just as many pages.

"What's that one about?" Ben asked, but Wesley was already too engrossed in the book to hear him.

They continued on.

And on.

And on.

The passageway twisted and split off into dozens of different tunnels. Paradise guided them through the maze, barely pausing at each junction they came to.

THE SHARK-Headed BEAR-Thing

"This way," she said, as they took yet another left along yet another corridor.

"I'm hungry," Ben said. "Is anyone else hungry?"

Without taking his eyes off his book, Wesley produced an apple from up his sleeve and passed it forwards.

"Thanks," said Ben. He raised the fruit to his mouth, but Paradise caught his arm and held it. She stopped walking and pressed a finger to her lips. With a tilt of her head she gestured towards the corner just ahead of them.

"We're almost there," she said. "He's just up ahead. We should stay quiet."

"Why?" asked Ben, taking a big crunchy bite of the apple. "I took care of the monster, remember? The Shark-Headed Bear-Thing

161

THE SHARK-Headed BEAR-Thing

is history. We don't have to worry about it any more," he said, and he stepped around the corner, holding the sun in a jar out in front of him.

He stopped again almost immediately. The grin fell from his face and his apple fell to the floor. He thought about taking a backwards step, but he knew it was already too late.

Behind him, he heard Paradise and Wesley both gasp.

Ahead of him, a whole gang of Shark-Headed Bear-Things turned their black eyes in his direction.

"But," he mumbled, "we should probably start worrying about these ones."

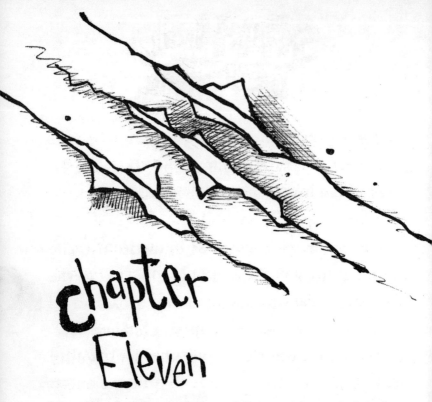

chapter Eleven

The Shark-Headed Bear-Things moved slowly. They advanced along the passageway towards the children, drool dangling from their jagged teeth. Some crawled on four legs, while others walked on two.

Ben counted the monsters. There were twelve of them, and not a lava river in sight.

THE SHARK-HEADED BEAR-Thing

There was no choice – they had to run.

"P-Paradise?" stumbled a voice from somewhere in the shadows beyond the beasts. Ben held up the jar and the darkness was pushed aside. A dishevelled figure hunched a little further along the tunnel, his face caked with dirt. "Paradise, is that you?"

"Mayor!" Paradise yelped. She darted towards him, but Ben caught her by the arm and pulled her back, just as the Bear-Things began to growl.

"No!" he said. "Stay back. We can't get to him."

"Let me go!" Paradise protested, but Ben kept his grip. He drew back as the monsters took another step closer.

"Wesley, can you do anything?"

Wesley hesitated. "Soil myself, possibly," he whispered.

"Come on," Ben urged. "Even a level one wizard must know *some* spells!"

"I ... I'm not sure," Wesley stammered. "I d-don't know."

Paradise rounded on him, desperation blazing in her eyes. "Do it! Whatever you can do, just do it! Please!"

Briefly, it looked like Wesley might burst into tears, but then he nodded. Ben and Paradise took another shuffled step back, but Wesley stayed where he was. He raised his hands and shot a nervous glance over his shoulder.

"You can do it," said Ben.

Wesley gave a cautious nod. "I ... I can do it."

His fingers began to dance as the shadows of the Bear-Things drew in around him. He could hear their breathing ringing loudly in the narrow space. He tried to ignore it, to push down his fears and remember his training.

"*Oyammi* ... what was it now?" he muttered. The growling of the monsters rolled off the walls on either side of him. "*Oyammi kerus* ... something ... *diddimus beyo*... thingy!"

Tiny yellow sparks spun like Catherine Wheels from the tips of his fingers. There was a *bang* and a puff of smoke. Ben and Paradise gazed on in wonder as a small amount of warm custard appeared in the air between Wesley and the Bear-Things. It seemed to hang there in empty space for a few seconds, then it fell with a *splat* to the floor.

THE SHARK-Headed BEAR-Thing

Wesley stared down at the yellow puddle. He swallowed nervously. "Or was it *diddimus bezo* thingy?" he wondered, before Ben shoved him out of the way.

"Cover your eyes!" Ben instructed. "You too, Mayor!"

Ben hurled the glass jar towards the monsters, then screwed his eyes shut and raised his arms in front of his face. There was a *smash*, then a *whoosh*, then the Shark-Headed Bear-Things began to squeal in shock.

Ben raced forwards. Even with his eyes closed, the light blazed through his eyelids and made his head throb. "Mayor," he called. "Where are you?"

"Over here!" cried the mayor, and Ben made for the direction of the sound.

"This way, follow my voice," he shouted to the others, pushing through the heaving mass of squealing Bear-Things. He expected them to grab for him, but they were obviously too busy with problems of their own. They writhed and thrashed and howled in pain. Their eyes, so used to the darkness of their underground tunnels, were burning in the blinding brightness.

Ben collided hard with the mayor, who immediately let out a high-pitched scream of fright. "Don't eat me! Don't eat me! I chew my own earwax!"

"It's me, Mr Mayor," Ben said. "I'm here to rescue you."

"*We're* here to rescue you," Paradise corrected, as she and Wesley stumbled through the thrashing knot of monsters.

"Oh, that's wonderful news!" the Mayor yelped. He fumbled for Paradise and hugged her tightly.

"Hooray for daring rescues! You're not hurt, are you, dear?"

"No, I'm fine. I'm fine."

The dazzle of the lights through Ben's eyelids had begun to fade a little, and the squeals of the Bear-Things were becoming more and more like growls again.

"Paradise!" said Ben. "Hate to break up the reunion, but we need a way out."

"On it," she replied. Even with her eyes shut, she could find the way. She could find *anything*.

"Take my hand," she told the mayor. "Ben, Wesley, take his other arm. Make a chain. Stay together."

The boys grasped around until they found the mayor. They hung on as Paradise led them

the first few faltering steps away from the Bear-Things.

The light was still fading. It had almost dimmed enough for them to open their eyes. Any second now, the monsters might recover.

"Quickly!" Wesley urged.

"If we run we might fall," Paradise said.

"If we don't run we'll *definitely* get eaten!" Wesley replied.

"I know which one I'd prefer," the mayor whimpered.

Paradise picked up the pace, but only a little. The monsters were no longer squealing and hissing in pain. They would still be dazzled, but that wouldn't last. Ben tried to open his eyes, but the fading glow of the tiny sun forced them shut again.

173

A moment later, Paradise pulled them round a corner and the shadows crept up to meet them. They blinked in the cool darkness, and patterns of light swirled across their vision.

Freshly dug soil and chunks of rock lay piled up in mounds around them. This tunnel looked brand new, as if it had only been dug

THE SHARK-Headed BEAR-Thing

within the last few hours. It opened out into a tall, cylinder-like cave that stretched up into blackness somewhere far above them.

Only it wasn't a cave, exactly. The walls weren't made of stone. They were made of packed dirt and tangled roots, and Ben shuddered when he saw a small army of bugs

squirming across them. From where he was standing, there didn't appear to be any other passageways leading away from the room.

"Well?" said Ben. "I thought you were taking us to the way out."

Paradise closed her eyes again, but only for a moment this time. She looked upwards. "There," she said. "The way out's up there."

"Great!" sighed Ben. "What are we supposed to do? Fly up?"

"Well, you're the big hero," Paradise replied. "You figure something out!"

"The stairs, perhaps?" suggested Wesley, squeezing between them. He pointed to a set of rough stone steps that had been cut into the curved wall.

The mayor made a run for it, racing towards

THE SHARK-Headed BEAR-Thing

the steps as fast as his legs would carry him. "Come on!" he yelped. "Before those things come back!"

The others set off after him, but Ben hung back. He frowned. "Stairs?" he muttered, and he found his eyes creeping over to a spot where the floor met the wall.

There was just enough light coming from the fading miniature sun to pick out the details of a small wooden chest, and a lump of rock with a piece of cloth draped over it.

Ben stared at the open chest.

He stared at his glove.

"Tavish's basement," he realised, looking up to the ceiling of shadow above him. "This is Tavish's basement. This is my house!"

chapter Twelve

Ben slowly approached the chest and the boulder with the blade buried in it.

"This way, hurry!" yelped Paradise, but he was still too shocked to hear her. It wasn't until the mayor let out a high-pitched scream of terror that he remembered what was happening. A monstrous shape came lumbering in from

THE SHARK-HEADED BEAR-THING

the tunnel. It staggered towards Ben, and he braced himself for the fury of its attack.

But it kept stumbling past him until its nose crunched against the far wall. It lashed out then, slashing at the wall with its claws and letting out a growl of frustration.

"It's still blinded," Ben realised, then he clamped his hand over his mouth as the Bear-Thing's head whipped around in his direction.

Ben looked up to where Paradise and the others were just visible halfway up the stairs. They were all gesturing in the direction of the tunnel mouth. Before he even turned, Ben knew what he would see. More of the monsters had found their way in. They shuffled around like the other one, their paws grasping at nothing.

THE SHARK-Headed BEAR-Thing

Meanwhile, the first monster was making its way towards him, its huge head cocked to one side, listening for the sound of his voice. Ben knew better, and was keeping his mouth firmly shut.

Paradise and Wesley beckoned for him to follow them up the stairs. Before he did, though, there was something he had to do.

As quietly as he could, he removed the cloth that was covering the hilt of the sword. He felt a jolt of excitement spread through him from the tips of his fingers to the ends of his toes as he wrapped his hand around the sword's handle.

This was it. He was ready. After everything he'd gone through, he knew he was ready!

He pulled.

The sword didn't budge.

He wasn't ready.

There was a *clunk* from somewhere in the shadows above him, followed by the loud *creak* of an old door being opened. Light trickled in, and Ben heard a familiar voice calling, "Hello? Is there someone down there?"

"Uncle Tavish," he said, then he immediately realised his mistake as a chorus of frenzied roars erupted around him. The Bear-Things lunged, clawing and swiping blindly in the direction the sound had come from.

Ben threw himself to the floor and used his elbows to crawl past them. The Bear-Things crashed together at the spot where he had stood, and lashed out at each other in blind rage.

THE SHARK-HEADED BEAR-Thing

Up above, the door closed with a *squeak* and a *slam*. "Uncle Tavish!" Ben bellowed, taking the stairs two at a time. "Open the door, open the door!"

The four of them bounded up the steps just as the rest of the Shark-Headed Bear-Things swarmed into the basement. The slapping of shoes on stone told the monsters all they needed to know. They charged up the stairs in pursuit, falling over one another in their race to the top.

"Uncle Tavish, it's me, open up!" Ben shouted. There was no point being quiet now. The shark-jaws were snapping at their heels, *clack-clack, clack-clack.* Any moment now Ben, Paradise and the others would be nothing more than a tasty between-meals snack.

The door was just five or six steps above them. It was still closed. Even if Tavish heard them now, there was no time for him to unlock and open it. Ben clenched the gloved hand into a fist, and this time he felt the metal quiver like it had done back at the bridge. A jolt of power tingled along his arm.

"OK, double-blooper," he said. "Let's see what you can do!"

Ben swung his fist at the door, hoping he

184

could somehow punch it open. Instead, a split-second before the gauntlet touched the wood, the door exploded into matchsticks. They all stumbled up the final few steps and out of the basement. Tavish was there, staring at them, his jaw hanging open and a cloud of sawdust slowly settling on top of his head.

"Ben?" he said. "How did you get down there? What did you do to my door? Why is there a massive monster running up the stairs?"

Tavish's eyes went wide. "Massive monster!" he yelped. "Running up the stairs!"

"You smashed the door!" Paradise cried. "Why did you smash the door?"

"It wasn't my fault, it was the glove!" Ben protested.

"Monsters! Monsters!" wept the mayor. He spotted Tavish looking at him, and hurriedly shook his hand. "The mayor of Loosh. Nice to meet you."

"Um ... you too," Tavish murmured.

The mayor flashed him a quick smile, then went back to screaming. "Monsters! Monsters! Don't let them eat me!"

"The glove," said Wesley below his breath.

With a hiss of hydraulics, Tavish's robotic arm scooped up a nearby workbench and pushed it in front of the doorway. He braced himself against it just as the first of the Bear-Things began to pound on the opposite side.

"*I'm just going to watch*, you said!" Tavish cried. "*I won't be in danger, I'm just going to watch!*"

THE SHARK-Headed BEAR-Thing

Ben shuffled awkwardly. "Um, yeah. That didn't quite go to plan."

"I noticed! This won't hold them for long," Tavish said. "Ben, get everyone to safety. Quickly!"

"I'm not going to leave you," Ben replied.

"Don't worry about me, I'll be fine," Tavish said. A monstrous paw splintered through the wood of the workbench, the claws swishing by just a few centimetres from his nose. "Oh no, my mistake. I'll be horribly killed, won't I?" Tavish realised. "This was a terrible plan!"

"The glove," said Wesley again, more loudly this time. "I know where I've seen the glove!"

He fumbled up his sleeve. "In here!" he cried, then he pulled out a pair of slippers shaped like cuddly kittens. "No, not in there,"

he sighed, shoving the slippers back up the sleeve. He pulled out a small notebook. "Here, the Journal of Thrugmud the Mad."

Wesley flipped through the pages. "I knew I'd seen it before. It first looked familiar back on the bridge when you grabbed me by the—"

"Hurry up!" bellowed everyone in the room, as the workbench continued to splinter and break.

"Yes. Sorry," said Wesley. He held up a

THE SHARK-Headed BEAR-Thing

double-page spread on which someone had sketched Ben's gauntlet in quite amazing detail. Hundreds of words were scribbled around the picture, but they were too jumbled and messy for Ben to make out.

"But what does it do?" Ben asked, but before Wesley could answer, the workbench was torn in two. Tavish swung with his robotic arm. His fist *clanked* against the first of the monsters, but this seemed only to make it angry. It pounced on the blacksmith, who barely had time to throw the arm up for protection.

Tavish clattered to the ground, the snarling Bear-Thing on top of him, pinning him down. The rest of the creatures poured out from the basement, snapping and growling, their black eyes now focused once more.

"Wesley, the glove!" Ben bellowed. "Tell me what it does!"

Wesley stepped up beside him. "This," he said, and he jabbed a thumb against a spot on the back of the gauntlet.

Ben's arm went numb. His whole skeleton began to vibrate. He clamped his teeth together, and as a buzzing filled his skull he heard Wesley shout at Paradise and the mayor to find something to hold on to.

His fingers tingled.

His skin crawled.

And something in the gauntlet went *WHOOSH*!

chapter Thirteen

Five beams of magical energy streamed from Ben's fingertips. They met at a point halfway across the room and suddenly there was a doorway there – a rectangular hole in the air itself, filled with a crackling purple light.

A wind whipped around the room. Ben's boots began to slip on the flagstone floor and he found himself sliding towards the hole. A hand snagged him before the doorway could pull him through.

"I've got you," said Paradise, shouting to make herself heard over the roaring wind. She, Wesley and the mayor were clinging to the Automated Breakfast Producing Device. Wesley helped Paradise heave Ben over to the contraption, and they all clung tightly to it as the hole in space became a swirling purple whirlpool.

"It's a portal!" Wesley bellowed. "The glove opens portals!"

"To where?" shouted Ben.

"I have no idea," Wesley admitted. "But not here, that's the main thing!"

They watched as, with a furious roar, the

monster closest to the portal was dragged through it. They saw its jaws gnash and

THE SHARK-Headed BEAR-Thing

its claws slash, and then it was gone.

Swords and hammers and horseshoes came spinning across the room and were sucked into the swirling vortex. The splintered remains of the workbench went next, followed by another of the Bear-Things.

And another, and another.

"It's working!" Paradise cried, as the remaining Shark-Headed brutes were dragged through one by one. "It's actually working!"

Down on the floor, Tavish was still wrestling with one of the creatures. The weight of his metal arm kept him safe from the portal's pull, but his shoulder was pinned and no matter how he tried to twist, he couldn't shove the Bear-Thing off.

With fumbling fingers, Tavish flicked a switch near the arm's elbow. "You're in trouble now," he announced, as the arm began to fold in on itself and transform. With a *hiss* of hydraulics, the arm turned into a small umbrella, which immediately turned inside out in the wind.

THE SHARK-HEADED BEAR-THING

"No, hang on, not that one," said Tavish, searching for a different switch.

Bellowing with rage, the monster reared up. A paw swatted the umbrella arm out of the way. The Bear-Thing's jaws opened wide, and then—

CLANG! A flying horseshoe struck it on the side of the head, stunning it. Tavish swung with his arm and the Bear-Thing went sprawling off him. The pull of the portal caught it, but this monster was larger than the rest. It dug its claws into the stone floor, and slowly, slowly, centimetre by centimetre, it began to crawl towards Ben and the others.

The building around them was shaking itself apart as the whirlpool began sucking the

stones from the walls. Ben and the others still had their grip on Tavish's machine, but they couldn't hold on forever, and the Bear-Thing was closing in.

Struggling with all his strength against the pull of the portal, Ben reached a hand up until he found a lever. "Hey, ugly," he yelled, yanking the handle down. "Breakfast is served!"

From inside the machine there came a surprised *cluck*. A split-second later, an egg was fired out at high-speed from somewhere within the machine. With the portal pulling on it, the egg travelled even faster than before. There was a loud *boom* as the egg became the first in history to break the sound barrier.

It exploded in a shower of shell and hot yolk against the Bear-Thing's head, and that was

THE SHARK-Headed BEAR-Thing

all it took for the monster to lose its grip. It flailed and flapped for not much time at all, and then through the portal it went.

"They're gone!" Wesley yelped.

"We're saved!" cheered the mayor.

"But how do I turn it off?" Ben cried. The howling of the wind whipped his words away, and the entire Automated Breakfast Producing Device began to tremble and shake.

Wesley's face went pale. "I forgot to check!"

"Well, check now!" said Paradise.

Wesley fumbled up his sleeve, and found the book, only for it to be torn from his grip and pulled through the portal. "Oops," he whimpered. "Butterfingers."

The whirlpool began spinning faster. They all cried out in fright as their feet were pulled

towards the hole, and their grips on the machine began to slip. "Try the same button again!" Wesley screamed, but Ben was holding on with both hands and couldn't reach the back of the glove.

"I have to let go," he announced.

"No!" gasped Tavish.

"Ben, don't!" Paradise cried, but it was too late. Ben opened his fingers and the portal caught him. He tumbled towards it, end over end, spinning and flipping as he fumbled his fingers over the back of the gauntlet, searching frantically for the button that would...

SHOOM!

With a final flickering flare-up, the whirlpool vanished. Ben clattered to the floor, bounced on his head, then rolled

THE SHARK-Headed BEAR-Thing

to a stop just where the portal had been.

For a moment, there was no sound in the room but the breathing of its five occupants. It was the Mayor of Loosh who finally broke the silence.

"Well," he breathed. "What an eventful day that was."

He opened his arms and Paradise threw hers around him in a hug.

"I knew you'd find me," the mayor said. "Even when I was down there with those things, I knew you'd find me."

"Why didn't they eat you?" Ben wondered.

"Do you know," said the mayor brightly, "I didn't think to ask?"

"And why were they coming here? Why were they digging into my basement?"

"Ah, now that I *did* ask them," replied the mayor.

"And?" said Ben. "What did they say?"

The mayor scratched his head. "If I recall correctly it was '*grrr raaar hsss grrr*'. Or words to that effect." He smiled broadly. "Don't worry about it, my boy. You've stopped them. It's over."

Tavish sat up suddenly. He took one look at the ruined remains of his house, then lay back down again, groaning.

"Oh, you poor chap," said the mayor. "Here, let me help you."

He rushed to the blacksmith's side, leaving Paradise with the two boys. "So … thanks," she said to Ben. "I couldn't have done it without you."

THE SHARK-HEADED BEAR-Thing

"You can say that again," Ben agreed.

Paradise glared at him. "Don't push it," she said. "Now I think about it, Wesley was probably more help than you were."

"Really?" asked Wesley, perking up.

"And all *he* did was magic up a bit of custard."

Wesley's shoulder sagged again. "I did warn you. Less magical ability than a sandwich."

"Hey, maybe not," said Ben. He stooped down and picked up a small metal box from among the debris on the floor.

"What's that thing?" asked Wesley cautiously.

Ben pointed one of the rectangular box's narrow ends at Wesley. "It's a magic detector," he explained. "One bloop means you're magic, two bloops means you're *really* magic."

"Three bloops means we're all about to die," Paradise added.

"It'll be three bloops then," said Wesley glumly. "Bound to be."

They all watched the box and waited.

And waited.

"Nothing. See, told you, I'm not magic," said Wesley, but then the end of the box flipped open, and the model bird popped out on its spring. The bird sat there for a while, trembling slightly.

THE SHARK-Headed BEAR-Thing

A moment later, it went *ptwing.*

A moment after that, its head exploded.

"Wh-what does that mean?" Wesley fretted.

Ben shrugged, then clapped his new friend on the shoulder. "No idea," he said, "but I bet it's going to be a lot of fun finding out."

Paradise gave them both a nod. "Well, I'll see you, I suppose."

"See you," Ben said.

"Hopefully not too soon," Paradise added.

Ben smiled. "Just what I was thinking."

Paradise looked down at the mayor, who seemed to be just finishing up a conversation with Tavish. "Are we ready to go?"

"Go?" the mayor replied. "*Go?* Oh my goodness, no! Mr Tavish and I have been talking, and what with Loosh being in ruins,

we're all going to need somewhere to live."

Paradise and Ben exchanged a glance. They both had a feeling they knew where this was going.

"So they're all going to come and stay here," said Tavish, letting the mayor help him to his feet. "The people of Loosh will move to Lump."

"Isn't it wonderful!" the mayor announced. "All of us together, like one big happy family!"

"Um … great," said Ben.

"Terrific," said Paradise.

The mayor put a hand on Ben's shoulder. "Mind if I have a word, young Benjamin?" he asked, steering Ben away from the others. When they were out of earshot, the mayor took Ben's hand and shook it. "You saved me

THE SHARK-Headed BEAR-Thing

today," he said. "You saved everyone."

"I didn't really do that much," replied Ben.

"Nonsense," the mayor said. He leaned in closer and lowered his voice a little. "Your parents would be proud."

Ben blinked in surprise. "You knew my parents?"

The mayor held his gaze for a while, then leaned back and shook his head. "I just meant … whoever they are. Whatever happened to them. They would have been proud."

He continued to look Ben in the eye, but gave a little nod of his head. "Nice glove, by the way. Very useful. Tell me … where did you get it?"

"Tavish found it," Ben said. "He found it with me when I was a baby."

"Ah," said the mayor. "In the wreckage?"

Ben began to nod, but then he stopped himself. "How did you know that? I didn't say anything about any wreckage."

"Oh no," said the mayor, "neither you did." He winked and smiled, then sauntered back over to continue his chat with Tavish. Ben watched the mayor for a while, then looked across his half-ruined home, to where Paradise and Wesley were trying to repair the magic detector. He stared down at his gauntlet and a tiny tickle tingled along his fingertips.

As he walked over to join his new friends, Ben couldn't shake the feeling that, after today, life was about to get a whole lot more interesting.

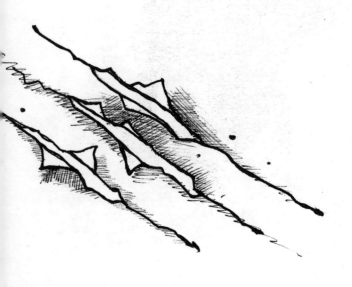

If you liked Benjamin Blank's
first adventure…

...then keep a beady eye out
for his next one...

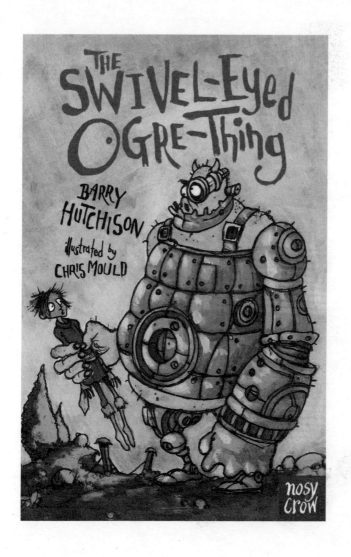

It's a real monster!